(1908–1980) was born in Por the daughter of a naval officer and an Ulster-Irish mother, she described her childhood as 'middle class and uneventful'. She came to London in her early twenties, after art-school training. She advanced from typing van-lists at Peter Jones for 15s a week to painting furniture, and then moved to book production at the Medici Society. Her friendship with Stevie Smith, bridesmaid at her wedding, dates from these times. Her first novel, *The Wind Changes* (1937), was published when she was twenty-nine.

A few days before war was declared she married R.D. Smith, then a British Council lecturer, later a distinguished radio producer, and Professor at the New University of Ulster and Surrey University. Olivia accompanied him to his post in Bucharest: from there they moved to Greece, and were evacuated to Egypt from Athens two days before the Germans put up their swastika on the Acropolis. Olivia was Press Officer to the United States Embassy in Cairo, and from 1941-45 worked in Jerusalem as Press Assistant at the Public Information Office in Jerusalem, and for the British Council.

After the war Olivia Manning established herself as one of Britain's foremost novelists. *Artist Among the Missing* was published in 1949, followed by *School for Love* (1951); *A Different Face* (1953); *The Doves of Venus* (1955); the Balkan Trilogy: *The Great Fortune* (1960), *The Spoilt City* (1962), *Friends and Heroes* (1965); *The Play Room* (1969); *The Rain Forest* (1974); and her Levant Trilogy: *The Danger Tree* (1977), *The Battle Lost and Won* (1978), and *The Sum of Things* (1980). She also published two volumes of short stories, a travel book on Ireland, a biographical study of Stanley in Africa, and a book on her much-loved Siamese and Burmese cats.

Olivia Manning lived for many years in St John's Wood, North London; she received the Tom-Gallon Trust Award in 1949 and was made a C.B.E. in 1976.

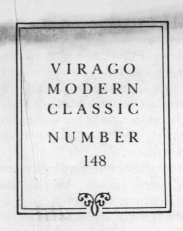

VIRAGO
MODERN
CLASSIC

NUMBER

148

THE
PLAY ROOM

Olivia Manning

With a New Introduction by
ISOBEL ENGLISH

Virago

Published by VIRAGO PRESS Limited 1984
20–23 Mandela Street, Camden Town, London NW1 0HQ

Reprinted 1986, 1990

First published in Great Britain by William Heinemann Limited 1969

Copyright © Olivia Manning 1969
Introduction copyright © Isobel English 1984

British Library Cataloguing in Publication Data
Manning, Olivia
The play room
I. Title
823'.914[F]   PR6063.A384
ISBN 0-86068-362-1

Printed in Great Britain by
BPCC Hazell Books
Aylesbury, Bucks, England
Member of BPCC Ltd.

To Jane and Jonathan
with love

INTRODUCTION

The Play Room, which is Olivia Manning's ninth novel, is also her shortest. When she had finished the Balkan trilogy in 1965, she was anxious to break new ground. She had in mind, too, that the book which she was going to write – about teenagers in the 1960s – might make a good film. In fact the film rights for *The Play Room* were bought by the producer Ken Annakin, and more than two thirds of it was completed before the money ran out. Olivia was disappointed but stoical. 'At least the novel got me on Desert Island Discs,' she said to me.

The central character in the novel is Laura Fletcher, a fifteen-year-old schoolgirl, who dreams of becoming a famous dramatist, with the collaboration of her younger brother Tom. In their back garden in North Camperlea, a rather seedy area of Portsmouth, she performs her own plays for the benefit of her father, a retired naval officer, who, 'solitary as Ludwig II in his private theatre', usually drops off after the first ten minutes.

At Buckland House School, where Laura is a day-girl, she longs to be popular and admired. Particularly she longs to be the Best Friend of Vicky Logan, who is beautiful, rich and kind-hearted in a rather indolent way. Once, when Laura was reduced to tears by the class bully, she had lent her a handkerchief: afterwards Laura, with an eye for the dramatic, had drawn a picture of her with a halo and written underneath – 'When all people rejected me, Victoria Logan lent me a handkerchief.' Laura's defensive methods are simple, if provocative. After reading a history of English literature, she claims to be descended from the Fletcher of Beaumont and Fletcher. She is naïve enough to think that this will make her more interesting and thus more sought-after by the other girls. Laura is painfully self-conscious about her lack of good looks: she is small and skinny, and her nose is too long and her chin too short. When she explodes to one of the mistresses 'Oh, Miss Lamb, I'm so ugly,' she really hopes to be reassured that this is not the case. But Miss Lamb tells her crisply that beauty is not everything – and Laura feels even more of a freak. Then, of course, Laura is a clever girl – clever and very literary. One morning she turns up at school with a copy of the *Times Literary Supplement* tucked under her arm, only to be jumped on by a girl in the form: 'Men don't like girls who read papers like that.' It was in fact Olivia's mother who had first warned her when she was a teenager of the dire consequences of being seen reading the *TLS*.

For the first five years of her life Olivia was the adored and cosseted only child of her parents. She was a bright and pretty little girl, only too willing to step forward and dance or recite to entertain her mother's friends. Then a terrible, and to Olivia inexplicable, change took place. After the birth of her brother Mrs Manning appeared to have no time for her daughter and to give all her attention to the new baby, who happened to be extremely delicate. Olivia felt the draught. At the age of five she had nothing to fall back on, no yardstick by which to measure the behaviour of adults. Because she felt she was no longer loved, she set about making herself into a difficult and most unlovable child. She became sullen and withdrawn, and whereas in the past she had inspired only praise and affection, she was now the cause of irritation and disapproval. But in spite of the disparity in their ages, there developed between brother and sister, as time went on, a closeness and affection for each other. This did not preclude a fair amount of bickering and teasing between them. As she told Kay Dick in *Friends and Friendship* (1974): 'He used to make fun of my nose – I never got over it.' What in reality Olivia never got over was the gut feeling of rejection by her mother, when her brother was born. Also, there was the indisputable fact of 'his amazing good looks'.

When *The Play Room* was published in 1969 Olivia Manning told a reporter from *The Guardian* that for the first time she had examined at length the relationship between herself and her brother when they were children. She had written briefly about him in some of her earlier short stories, but not until the present novel had she analysed the fits of jealousy that she had felt as a child, which on one occasion had almost precipitated murder. 'I tried to murder you once,' Laura Fletcher tells her brother Tom. He is good-natured and disbelieving – but nonetheless curious. Laura then proceeds to explain how, when he was a baby, she had planted a thermos flask on the stairs to trip her mother up as she came down carrying him.

The story is a true one. But if Olivia was envious of her brother, she was also proud of him. When he was killed in 1941 on active service in the Fleet Air Arm, she was deeply distressed. She wrote to me some thirty years later of the terrible shock that it had been to her parents, and how helpless she had felt at the time since she was stranded in Egypt: 'On my return to England, after the war, whenever my mother got me to herself, she would start talking about it – and I simply could not bear it. Sometimes I . . . walked away . . . My father suffered even more. He was very sensitive, and when the news came through of my brother's death, he sank into a chair and became completely silent. He did not speak to anyone for more than a year afterwards.'

In 1947 Olivia dedicated her second book *The Remarkable Expedition* to her brother with these words: 'He has no grave but the sea.' Lieutenant Oliver Manning had been drowned near the Nabb Tower, off the Isle of Wight.

To Olivia and her brother the Isle of Wight seemed always to be 'another world, a paradise'. When they were children living in Portsmouth, they would gaze across the stretch of water to the island with a sense of wonder. In their minds they associated it with the Irish Isles of the Blest, which they had seen when staying with their mother's relations in County Clare and Galway. In June 1970 Olivia wrote to me about a visit that we had made to Alum Bay: 'I often think of that wonderful afternoon we had there with the very delicate mist hanging over everything and the foghorn going and our trip round the Needles. All the summers of one's life add up in the end to a few exquisite days like that.'

When the children were young, the family used to go on day trips to the Isle of Wight. Money was fairly tight, and even the fare on the ferry was a strain. Disembarking at Ryde, they would walk along the coast to Seaview and then catch the bus to Bembridge for a picnic. There was never enough time in one day to explore the interior of the island, or to climb St Catherine's Down or see the Needles. All during their childhood the famous coloured sands at Alum Bay had to be taken on trust.

The first part of *The Play Room* describes a week's holiday that Laura and Tom spend on the Isle of Wight at Easter. Laura, in a desire to assert her independence, has set the whole thing in motion. Without telling her mother, she has followed up an invitation to go and stay with Mrs Button, a cleaner who once worked for them and has now retired to the island. Mrs Button has kept up with the family each Christmas, always writing in her card:

> Best of cheer from Mrs B.
> Won't you come and stay with me?

She is nevertheless surprised when her invitation is taken literally. When Laura's mother discovers what her daughter has been up to, she is furious: 'You're as deceitful as your father.' But after shouting and raving, she gives in on the condition that Tom accompanies his sister, which is not really what Laura, in her bid for freedom, has in mind. Mrs Fletcher also smoothes the children's path with the slightly reluctant Mrs Button by sending her two five-pound notes to help towards their keep.

When Laura and Tom arrive at Mrs Button's cottage it is nearly dark. Mrs Button is dressed to go out: she greets them casually, then plonks a plate of ham and tomatoes in front of them and pushes off to meet her 'friend' at the pub. Laura is dazzled by the glamour of the spare bedroom, with its pink plastic shelves over the hand-basin and the neon-lit mirror. Tom is quite happy to double up on the sofa in the living room.

The next morning Mrs Button makes it clear that she does not expect them home until the evening. They are entirely free to explore and go where they like. On the last day of the holiday they take the bus to Alum Bay. Tom is at first disappointed with the muted colours of the sands — rose-pink, rose-brown, slate-grey and violet-grey. He has expected a much more violent collection of colours. But when Laura points out a boss of yellow, 'rich as Solomon's gold', his excitement returns. 'I bet I can climb up there,' he says. However the yellow rock proves inaccessible.

Wandering along the shore towards Totland Bay, they are cut off by the incoming tide and have to scramble up the steep and crumbling cliff-face. They arrive unexpectedly on the edge of a private garden surrounding a large house. A peculiarly dressed lady sees them from the french windows and beckons. 'Come a little closer,' she calls. 'I won't hurt you.'

She is certainly weird, but she does show a great interest in the children and is very flattering about Tom's good looks and reassuring to Laura about hers: she tells her that she is *jolie-laide* and that if she were in Paris they would make a cult of her. Laura is deeply flattered. Because Mrs Toplady (as she introduces herself) has taken such a shine to the children, she offers to show them her play room. It is in an outbuilding in the garden, with a heavy padlock on the door. Tom anticipates a wonderful display of model trains and cars. When the door is opened he cannot see very clearly into the room in the fading afternoon light – but what he does see disturbs him and makes him want to run away. Laura is braver and more curious. She peers into the room, trying to pick out what is happening amongst the group of huge dolls with no clothes on. Mrs Toplady watches the children carefully for their reactions – and offers to wind up the dolls to make them move. Tom begins to yell and throw himself about for which he gets a slap on the head from Mrs Toplady. He runs screaming down the long drive with Laura on his heels.

Back at school for the summer term, Laura feels her experience of freedom during the holidays, particularly her experience of Mrs Toplady's play room, will give her status in the eyes of Vicky Logan and her Best Friend Gilda

Hooper. She is right, too. From being merely an oddity on the outside, Laura becomes gradually accepted as a member of the trio. She is even invited to tea at Vicky's rather smart house in South Camperlea – the expensive end of Portsmouth. When Gilda goes abroad for the summer holidays with her family, she delegates Laura to look after Vicky for her while she is away.

When Olivia was writing *The Play Room* she was anxious to find out all that she could about discos from the teenage daughters of friends like myself. She even thought of going on her own to a disco in search of first-hand experience. A kind of adventurousness came over her, which manifested itself in an unexpected way.

In the late spring of 1968 Olivia and her husband Reggie spent a few days in Cowes with me. I had also staying in the house my daughter and a nineteen-year-old American cousin. Olivia took a fancy to Paul – perhaps because he brought back memories to her of her dead brother. She wrote to me afterwards: 'My brother was exceptionally good-looking, although he did not have the absolute beauty of Paul . . .'

One afternoon we took Paul to see the Roman villa at Newport. It is situated in a suburban road. 'Shades of Stevie Smith,' said Olivia when she noticed that it was called Avondale Road.* Apart from the signs and arrows pointing to the entrance, there was nothing to suggest that the corrugated iron building was anything more than an ordinary shed. The place was bolted and barred and there was no one about. Neither Olivia nor Paul were put off by this, and quick as a flash they were over the fence and scrambling up onto the ledge of the shoulder-high window.

*Stevie Smith lived at 1 Avondale Road, Palmers Green, in North London.

With the help of Olivia's nail file and Paul's strong wrists, the window was soon unfastened, and we squeezed through, dropping down onto the concrete walk which surrounded the whole excavation. Before leaving, we followed Olivia's example and put our entrance money in the box by the door.

Laura in the novel has much of the young Olivia in her. She is a mixture of fearlessness and timidity. She is prepared to go along with Vicky in her escapades to discos in the rougher areas of Portsmouth, not so much because she enjoys it, but because it is what Vicky wants. Vicky is a born, if languid, exhibitionist, and Laura looks on with awe and admiration as she chances her arm, and becomes more and more deeply involved with Clarrie, an uneven-tempered and disturbing youth from a nearby factory. Laura is afraid of Clarrie and cannot really understand what it is that attracts Vicky to him. But Vicky is hellbent on her own elaborate game of chasing and being chased. When Laura is pushed into dancing with Clarrie she tries to make conversation. 'We've got a cat called Sugarpuss,' she says inconsequentially – and draws a complete blank.

Olivia came down to the Isle of Wight for the last time on 4 July 1980. She was staying with her devoted friends Parvin and Michael Laurence, whose house at Billingham had become a second home to her. She brought with her, as always, her Burmese cat, who was seventeen years old.

Although I was at the time in Cowes, I did not know of Olivia's visit until the day after she arrived, when Michael telephoned to say that she had had a stroke. Later in the afternoon he took us to see her in hospital. The four of us crowded into the small white room, with the blinds half drawn. Olivia was rather sleepy at first, and seemed not to know what had happened to her. Then she began to worry about her cat. 'What about my poor Miou?' she asked – and I offered to look after him until she was better. She became more pulled together as she explained to me that Miou could only eat plaice fillets for his breakfast and poached turkey breasts for his tea. When she had got that straight, she was suddenly sad to think that she would miss the Christina Foyle Literary Lunch to which, for the first time in her life, she had been invited as a special guest. She very much wanted Parvin to bring in her make-up case the next day. Then she grew silent as if she had had enough of us. I remember holding her hand and the firmness of her grip. When she spoke again her voice was as strong and as forceful as it had ever been. 'Don't hang about. If you're waiting for a train to go, go *now*.' These were the last words I heard her speak.

Olivia Manning died on 23 July at the Royal County Hospital in Ryde. Her death was reported the following week in the local paper, where she was described as 'Olivia Manning – the Isle of Wight novelist.' The island had finally claimed her for its own.

Isobel English,
Cowes, 1983.

I

THE ISLAND

Gilda Hooper, wedged with her Best Friend into a small front desk, was comparing the boys of Camperlea. She spoke as an authority on male shortcomings. There was scarcely a Grammar School boy she had not found wanting, and she had tried all of them: or so she said. The one she derided most was Bobby Bonham.

Examinations had ended that morning. The five exam-passing girls in the back row were subdued, like runners who have run a race but must still await the judges' decision. It was the last afternoon of term and anyone could talk who wished. With the Head Girl tolerant, no one tried to interrupt Gilda who was, in any case, intimidating.

Her friend, Vicky Logan, was a beauty. Vicky had never tried to pass an examination in her life. Everyone knew that should she choose to earn her living, she could at once become a film star or a model or something like that. Gilda claimed to know everything about sex but Vicky, who did not claim anything, was thought to know more.

'Bobby Bonham,' said Gilda, 'is too dim to live.'

'So much for Bobby Bonham!' murmured the Head Girl.

Gilda screamed: 'But he's a drag. Isn't he, Vicky? Vicky, isn't Bobby Bonham a drag?'

Vicky, lying across the desk-top, her face on her arm, smiled and said: 'Poor Bobby. The sad thing is, he's mad about girls.' She sipped the blue vein of her inner arm, then giggled: 'He's mad to have a girl of his own. He wouldn't care who it was. Really. He'd have anyone.' Indolently moving her head, she surveyed the girls behind and her gaze settled on Laura Fletcher: 'He'd even have you, Laura.'

Laura, gratified at being noticed, scarcely taking in what Vicky had said, was puzzled by Gilda's laughter. When some of the others laughed, she joined in, pretending it was a joke: but the remark was with her all the way home. By the time she reached Rowantree Avenue, it had burrowed down into her most secret and vulnerable self. She was forced to confront it. She had to see it for what it meant. It meant that Vicky and Gilda and the others thought her so abject a creature that no one would look at her. Ever. Except perhaps that dim-witted Bonham or Hen Clarke whom she hated.

Pierced by Vicky's cruelty, she could scarcely hold back her tears. Yet Vicky was not a cruel girl. Laura had not immediately grasped the import of the remark because of Vicky's known kindness. She had been kind to Laura when Laura was being tormented by the terrible Hilda Small-piece. In those days Laura was always inventing some romantic story about herself. She had told the Lower School that she had a nursery and a nurse and a governess and the other appurtenances that children had in story-books. Later, when history took a hold on her, she pretended she had had interesting ancestors. The Lower School had dismissed her as 'batty'. When she rose into the Intermediate, she did not get off so lightly. Reading ahead in *The History of English Literature* she had been

4

struck by the names Beaumont and Fletcher, and at once claimed descent from John Fletcher.

Hilda, a senior girl but not a back-row senior, had decided to take the matter up. Sauntering into the Intermediate at Break, she said in a high, fluting voice, 'So we have some very important ancestors, have we?' and made clear who was the selected victim by giving Laura's hair a tweak. The tweak was so sharp that Laura's eyes filled with water and she was at a disadvantage from the start.

The other girls at first were fearfully silent but when Hilda started to posture and keep up that ridiculous voice, they had to laugh.

'Oh, Ah've got very important ancestors, too,' said Hilda. 'Dear me, yers. Vey-ray, vey-ray important! Adam and Eve were meh ancestors, don't you know!'

Laura's room-mates began to titter and Hilda, encouraged, gave a lecture on family trees: 'So useful, a family tree-hee! You can hang anything on it. I wouldn't be without one,' and so on and on, with Laura's hair tweaked at every sentence.

The others laughed and Valerie Whittam, Laura's then Best Friend, laughed the most: only Laura wept. It was not just the hair-tweaking, though that was demoralizing enough; it was the sense of being helpless and alone before this terrible enemy. And she was alone. A victim, it seemed, had no friends, though later Valerie excused her laughter by saying. 'She really is funny, you know. She's just like the comics on the pier.'

However much Laura tried to control herself, she would always end as a snivelling wreck. And her collapse had an odd effect on Hilda who would at once become unfunny and personal. 'Oh, boo-hoo-ho!' she would mimic Laura. 'Look at me! My daddy's a naval officer, my daddy is.

Ever so brave, he is! We're a cut above common shop-keeping people, we are!'

At this, Laura would weep the more because it was so unfair. The Smallpieces owned a radio shop for which Laura might well envy them. They lived near the sea, which the Fletchers did not. Laura, brought up amid economies, had thought the Smallpieces rich; but Hilda had illusions about the naval community. She towered over Laura, who was small for her age, and beat her down with accusations: 'You think you're someone because your father was an officer, but he wasn't always an officer. He began by swabbing the decks.'

'He didn't. He didn't,' howled Laura.

'Oh, yes, he did. Oh, yes, he did.'

Although there were other girls in the room whose fathers had risen from petty officer to officer, there was not one who dared stand up to Hilda. Her performance was repeated each day at Break. Laura used to feel sick as this time of torture approached. The teacher who came in after Break must have seen Laura puffy-eyed and sniffing, but nothing was said. A long time afterwards, when Hilda and Hilda's inflamed venom had sunk into the past, Miss Lamb spoke of it to Laura: 'I know you used to be unhappy here, Laura, but you brought it on yourself.'

Vicky, also in the Intermediate, was away at this time because of her brother's death and her mother's illness. When she came back and for the first time witnessed Hilda cavorting and cackling and tweaking Laura's hair, she seemed bewildered. There was nothing she could do, of course. Though she was a year older than Laura, she was four or five years younger than Hilda: but at the end, when Laura was left in a despairing huddle, she said with

6

firm kindliness: 'Come on. Sit up and dry your eyes before Miss Lamb comes in.' When Laura opened her hand to show that her handkerchief was a ball of tears, Vicky threw her own clean handkerchief on to Laura's desk. It was a casual gesture but Laura, like a tortured prisoner shown unexpected kindness, had felt a luxurious desire to kiss Vicky's feet.

Those days were over now, thank goodness. Hilda, who never became a back-row senior, left that summer and now she was nothing but a white-faced gargoyle stuck in the cash-desk of her father's shop and glowering out of the window at the passers-by. What remained, was Laura's admiration for Vicky and for her nobility, that seemed a natural adjunct of beauty. Though Vicky had done nothing to encourage it, this admiration had grown. When Laura brought the handkerchief back, saying proudly 'It's been washed', Vicky replied 'So I should hope' and pushed it indifferently out of sight.

Laura herself became a senior, the youngest member of the Upper School, and the Head Girl told her, in the greatest confidence, that Miss Lamb had said: 'I am pleased to see Laura Fletcher is becoming a Character rather than a Freak.'

Over the years, observant and admiring, Laura had noted how Vicky remained aloof from schoolroom pettiness so she seemed to Laura above human weakness; one to whom, if need be, appeal could be made.

Laura had defended Vicky's beauty when critics argued that because her eyes were green instead of blue, her hair ashen instead of gold, Vicky was less than perfect. Laura, respected in this matter because she was good at drawing, insisted that green and silver-gilt were colours more subtle in their appeal than blue and butter-yellow. Remembering the passion of her defence, Laura was overwhelmed by the thought of Vicky's ingratitude.

But she had to get home. She had to face her mother. Blinking her eyes to keep from crying, she saw she was near the double cherry that had replaced old Mr Newton's monkey-puzzle tree. The infant cherry, no bigger than Laura herself had produced three coronals of buds and the buds were already shaking out petals of crumpled silk. Easter was late and she and Tom were going to the Island. Though she had been injured beyond bearing, life had not ended yet.

Laura was home early but her mother jumped up at the sight of her, saying in relief: 'So there you are!' as though she had perhaps been killed by a bus or raped in broad daylight. 'Tom's in. I'll wet the tea. Let's get it over.' Anxious to force time along, Mrs Fletcher hurried to the kitchen where the kettle was murmuring over a low gas. Returning with the teapot, she told Laura to call Tom down from his room. After Laura had shouted up the stairs, Mrs Fletcher impatiently asked: 'Is he coming? Is he coming? You sit down, anyway, Laura. I hate this hanging about.' She ignored her husband who was drowsing by the fire with the cat on his knee.

'Is that boy coming?' she asked as the door opened; then, as Tom appeared: 'Didn't you hear your sister call?'

Tom, never impressed by his mother's agitation, calmly said 'I was washing my hands', and started to butter his bread.

The tea-table floated in silvery shadow. Though outdoors it was still bright, the light could make little headway through the coloured window-panes, the lean-to conservatory and the lanky geraniums that pressed against the glass.

But it was too early to turn on the light; besides, Mrs Fletcher liked the half-light. With her children safely back and at the table, she felt that the day's harassment was nearly over. For a while there was peace but Laura, the complainer, was plotting more complaints.

She was putting her troubles down to the fact she lived in Rowantree Avenue. It was, she decided, the longest and dreariest road in Camperlea and in the whole of its long, dreary length there was not one presentable boy of the right age. No wonder she was relegated to some outcast from another part of town! No wonder they thought she would do for Bobby Bonham!

When she had not been invited to Gilda Hooper's Christmas party, she concluded it was a case of out-of-sight, out-of-mind. Living half-way down this mile-long road, she was always too far away. How could she hope to participate in the great events of life? When this had first occurred to her, she asked why on earth her parents ever thought of coming to live here.

She was told they had married in the early fifties when there were few houses to be found. Camperlea, a residential neighbour of Portsmouth, had suffered for its nearness to the naval dockyard. Half the houses were damaged and still unrepaired. 'We had to be glad to get anything,' said Mrs Fletcher.

'But that was years ago,' Laura protested: 'There's nothing to stop us moving now.'

'Oh, yes, there's plenty to stop us. We can't afford the new houses and we wouldn't get much for this one. Besides, there's the mortgage. That's not paid up yet.'

Laura now, her frustrations the more clamorous because of Vicky Logan's remark, looked round the room with dislike. If they did have to live here, they did not have to live with cream distemper. 'What we need is wallpaper,' she said.

Her mother was amazed. 'Wallpaper was old-fashioned even when I was a girl.'

'Oh, Mummy, you're hopeless. Everybody in London has wallpaper.'

'I don't care what they have in London. We like the room as it is.'

Mrs Fletcher would never change anything. Though Laura argued, she knew that argument was a waste of breath. Conditions at 201 Rowantree Avenue were inflexible. If she wanted to change her surroundings, she must do it by walking out of here.

Vicky had been right. If she remained in Camperlea Laura would end up with someone like Bobby Bonham or Hen Clarke. She blamed her mother for it. She would, she felt, have been a totally different person had she not been born in this dreary town, in this dreary avenue and in a house perpetually fretted by the winds of anxiety.

Mrs Fletcher, daughter of a stern father whom she tried to imitate, came from a Baptist family and an isolated country area. The war had brought her to work in Portsmouth dockyard but it had not changed her. She had married out of the faith but the small community outlook still possessed her.

Years ago Laura said to Valerie Whittam: 'You think your mother is twenty years out of date! My mother is fifty years out of date. In fact, she's a hundred years out of date. She's not just pre-war, she's pre- the war before that. And she's so obstinate, you can do nothing with her.'

Though spoken from nothing but the insight of childhood, that, Laura thought, was true. All Laura could hope for was to start from the beginning again. She might start by changing her name.

She said suddenly: 'Why wasn't I christened Sarah?'

'Sarah!' Mrs Fletcher sounded as though she could not believe her ears. 'I had a great-aunt called Sarah and a bitter old pill she was.'

Laura could only smile, certain the name of her mother's aunt did not relate in any way to the name carried by the Head Girl at Buckland House School. She added: 'Or Victoria?'

'Like the railway station,' said Tom.

Mrs Fletcher made a derisive noise: 'Who would want to be called Victoria?'

'Who would want to be called Laura?'

Strangely enough, this daring retort did not affect her mother but it roused her father to gentle rebuke: 'Laura,' he said, 'is your mother's name.'

His wife turned on him: 'If you want your tea, you'll put that cat down and come to the table. I'm not giving you a tray over there.'

'Oh, dear! Oh, dear!' Easing himself up and easing Sugarpuss down with the minimum of shock, he grumbled humorously: 'No rest for the wicked.' Sugarpuss fell, clinging to the beloved knee till he could cling no longer, then, on the hearth-rug, giving vent to indignation by stabbing at his fur with his tongue. Mr Fletcher, pink-faced from the fire, came to the table murmuring 'Poor Sugarpuss! Poor old fellow!', lavishing compassion on the cat and all else, himself included.

Tom and Laura had shown no surprise at their father's treatment. They knew he had lost all standing in the house. And he had lost it deservedly. He had once given away a

11

thousand pounds. It had happened a long time ago when he retired from the Navy.

He had retired and married about the same time. When on active service, he had crowds of friends and never thought of marriage. 'He was having too good a time,' Mrs Fletcher said with a significant nod. When he took Tom and Laura out on Sunday walks, he told them much the same thing. Naval life, he said, was just what he wanted. He was always off somewhere and when he came back, full of experiences and funny stories, he was welcome everywhere. The only bills he had to worry about were mess bills and his account with the naval tailor on Portsmouth Hard. He dressed well. He was a handsome man, not tall but well built and light on his feet. When he married, even though late in life, it came as a shock to a number of women. People were always telling Mrs Fletcher how popular he had been at naval dances where he swept round the floor on his light dancing feet. That did not please her much. 'He was getting past it when I met him,' she said, and she often hinted to Laura that a woman was unwise to marry a man much older than herself. He had married as a safeguard against shore life with its household worries and he chose Mrs Fletcher because, unlike most of his women friends, she was a sober, moral young woman who could do accounts. The thousand pounds had been his terminal grant on retirement. Unused to matrimony, he saw the money as a gift to do what he liked with and when his old friend Penny Singleton asked if he might borrow it, he lent it without a thought. Penny Singleton said he would double it but that was the last Mr Fletcher saw of his money. Penny Singleton rented the old Officers' Club on Camperlea front, gutted it and started an amusement arcade. The residents of South Camperlea sent in a protest to the Town Council and the arcade was closed down. Penny Singleton, burdened with debts, swam out to the end of the pier and let himself sink to the bottom.

'Does the arcade belong to us now?' Tom asked when he first heard this story.

'No, it does not,' his mother replied. 'It belongs to the ground landlord but it's a white elephant anyway. Penny Singleton never paid the rent. Money ran through his fingers like water. I can't think why they called him "Penny" for he never had one.'

Mrs Fletcher had not known about the thousand pounds until years later when her friend, Mrs Vosper, said that the terminal grant had risen dramatically. 'Your husband,' she said, 'only got a thousand. But that Hooper with his Maltese wife will get three thousand or more.' Mrs Fletcher suffered, at one and the same time, the loss of the money and the fact she had not known it existed. 'To think,' she would say, 'he never told me. I had to learn about it from strangers.'

Laura felt the only thing to be done with so dire a happening was to suppress it, but Mrs Fletcher felt quite differently. Her husband would shift in his chair and look shamefaced and when at the end she said, 'To think he never told me,' he would try and laugh it off. He meant, he said, to tell her when the money was doubled; then he would have given it all to her.

As for Mr Hooper and his three thousand! 'What did he do to deserve three thousand, I'd like to know?' said Mrs Fletcher. 'And when he gets it, he won't be such a fool as to lend it. You mark my words.' She was right. Mr Hooper took over the arcade and filled it with deck-chairs which he rented to summer visitors. He opened a newspaper shop and sold sweets and toys. When this prospered, he started the Select Tea Rooms. 'He's a natural businessman,' Mrs Fletcher said, admiring in spite of herself: 'He's coining.' All Mr Fletcher did was get a job with a firm that hired out slot machines. Everybody liked him and found it easy to cheat him. During the war he had been injured in the cheek by a piece of flak. The wound healed, so he received no disability pension, but his eye ached and watered when he was tired. He also suffered from bronchitis. By the time he was sixty, he was not well enough to go out in all weathers to collect money from the slot machines. He retired again and came home to do a share of the housework.

As the room dissolved in its own shadows, the glasswork took on ecclesiastical splendour. There was a whole row of windows looking into the conservatory but only a small area of each was designed to admit light. In the centre of each window a country scene was burnt in sepia, then came a surround of clear glass, then borders of red, blue and yellow squares, a medley without order, the panes put in as they had come to hand.

Laura, the art authority of Buckland House School, decided that the whole arrangement was beneath contempt; yet almost until that very moment she had accepted her mother's belief that the coloured glass was an adornment and the pride of the house. Mrs Fletcher often spoke of the pleasure she had felt when, with so much destroyed in the world, she had first seen the windows intact. Their survival enriched them for her and gave them value. At one time Laura, imbued with her mother's admiration, had told

people they had the most beautiful windows in Camperlea. All that was a long time ago, so long that, remembering
it, there came over Laura a sense of sweet intimacy that
belonged to a past so remote it had no more definition
than a dream. She knew from hearsay that she had once
been a spoilt only child, her mother's adored baby, so
pretty and charming that people said 'What a charming
little girl!' Mrs Fletcher used to complain: 'I don't know
what's come over you. You used to be such a clever little
thing,' but she had given that up. Obviously Laura would
never be pretty, charming and clever again, and Mrs
Fletcher now placed her hopes in Tom who had inherited
his father's good looks.

Oh well! Laura rejected was Laura free. Had she remained an only child, she would have been trapped like
poor Miss Everest who pushed her mother up and down
Rowantree Avenue in a wheel-chair.

'We might have the light on,' said Mrs Fletcher and
Mr Fletcher, whose sight was poor, snapped it on before
she could think again. Tom, given light to see, began a
syrup picture on his slice of bread and butter. He was a
placid boy except for moments when panic came down on
him. Laura let him complete his drawing of an aircraft,
then whispered, 'The Island.'

Glancing up sharply, he raised his brows in inquiry
and Laura shrugged, suggesting that difficulties had
arisen.

His face grew taut and he cried in alarm: 'Aren't we
going then?'

Mrs Fletcher, alerted, did not know what the trouble
was but automatically gave Laura a threatening stare.

'Aren't we going?' Tom persisted.

'Going where?' asked his mother.

'To stay with Mrs Button.'

'We'll see. If there are any more complaints or arguments you won't go a foot.'

'But it's arranged. *When* are we going?'

'Thursday,' Laura said.

'Are we? Are we? Are we going on Thursday?'

'I suppose so,' Mrs Fletcher sighed. 'Though why you want to go and stay with that woman I don't know.'

Year after year Mrs Button, who once worked for Mrs Fletcher, had sent a Christmas card with the words:

'Best of cheer from Mrs B.
Won't you come and stay with me?'

No one had taken the invitation seriously until last Christmas Laura, thinking 'Why not?', wrote and suggested an Easter visit. The Isle of Wight was not far but it was a first step away from the restraints of home. Weeks passed before a reply came and the letter, lacking enthusiasm, had caused uproar in the Fletcher household. 'You're as deceitful as your father,' Mrs Fletcher shouted at Laura and Laura, who had imagined herself impressing everyone by her independent action, became frightened at what she had done. Mrs Fletcher raged for two days, then collapsed. 'Let her go. Let her know what it's like to live among strangers.'

This was no triumph for Laura. Her mother's dire tone made the visit sound like a death sentence. Only her own obstinacy kept her from cancelling all arrangements.

'*But*,' said Mrs Fletcher, 'you don't go alone. Not at your age.'

'Oh, Mummy, really! I'm fifteen. Lots of girls go away alone at fifteen.'

'I don't care what lots of girls do. You don't go alone. Tom will go with you.'

Tom, having kept outside the tumult, was not over-eager to be drawn into it. He did not think he wanted to go and stay with Mrs Button. Mrs Button, who was really Miss Button, had been a humble, apologetic creature when they knew her, sole guardian of an illegitimate son, grateful for everything Mrs Fletcher gave her. He did not expect much fun with Mrs Button.

He and Laura only knew the north coast where they had been taken on children's outings. Mrs Button's cottage, bought for her by her son Cyril, was somewhere on the southern half of the Island. Laura began to extol the south coast as a place of legend and mystery, full of natural marvels. There were great cliffs where headlands broke free without warning and tumbled down to the sea. At one time the sea road had been cut through and part of it had slipped down to the shore taking with it all the houses and trees and rocks. You could still see the edge over-hanging the gulf. And there was tropical foliage. Laura had read all this in the library guide.

'Tropical?' Tom's large, dark eyes began to gleam with interest. 'Jungle? Bananas and coconuts?'

'Not exactly jungle, but palms. And there've been ship-wrecks. There's a museum full of shipwrecks. And there's a chine with smugglers.'

'There aren't any smugglers nowadays.'

'That's where you're wrong. There are smugglers. They pull into the chine at night. They come from France with all sorts of things. It's fan-*tas*-tic.'

When Tom had been won to the visit, Mrs Fletcher's opposition reasserted itself in a new form. She had hoped Laura would voluntarily change her mind and had imagined her saying 'I don't want to leave you, Mummy darling,' or 'If you don't want me to go, then I won't go.' Having waited in vain for Laura's capitulation, she suddenly said in a persuasive tone: 'You don't want to go and stay with that woman Button, do you?' Laura could not speak for exasperation and Mrs Fletcher, mistaking her silence, went on calmly: 'I've been thinking about it. I don't trust that woman and I don't like you children going there and not knowing where you're going. There are always a lot of strangers over there at Easter. You never know who might pick you up.'

'*Pick us up!* Oh, Mummy, really!'

'I'm speaking for your own good. You shouldn't want to go. You're a girl. You ought to know better.'

'Why ought a girl to know better?'

'Because she ought.'

'How silly can you get!'

Mrs Fletcher then appealed to Tom, speaking in the confiding, honeyed voice she used when they were alone together: 'Mummy's little boy doesn't want to go to the Island, does he? He doesn't want to leave his mother. I'll write a note to Mrs Button and tell her . . .'

'But I do want to go,' Tom interrupted coldly.

Denied, Mrs Fletcher changed tactics; the change was dramatic. With voice rising into an eerie howl, she said: 'Go, then, go. If you want to leave your poor mother who has given her life to looking after you, go . . . go . . . go . . .'

Neither Tom nor Laura could bear this. Laura cowered under it but Tom opened his mouth and screamed:

'Stop it. Stop it. Stop it.'

Mrs Fletcher seemed to wake up with surprise. 'All right,' she sharply said as one who could do no more. 'Go

18

if you want to go. And if anything happens to you, don't blame me.'

'Now,' said Mrs Fletcher when tea was over, 'I'll clear the table and Laura can help her father wash up.'

'And what will Tom do?' Laura sweetly asked.

'He'll do his homework.' Tom did not break up until Wednesday.

'Tom has all week-end to do his homework. Let him help Daddy for a change.'

Mrs Fletcher sighed deeply. She was weary of Laura's protests.

She had loved her domineering father and sought his likeness in her husband. Though her husband had proved a double disappointment – being, in her opinion, a fool and an old fool – she still saw the male as a privileged creature. Her husband had lost his privileges, of course, and with good reason, but she still accorded them to Tom. 'You don't ask a boy to wash dishes,' she said. 'You'll have a house of your own one day. You have to learn to be a housewife.'

'Oh! And is Tom learning to be a carpenter?'

'A carpenter!' To Mrs Fletcher the idea was so absurd, she merely smiled: 'I don't think Tom wants to be a carpenter.'

'No. *Ex*-actly. And I don't want to be a housewife.'

'Oh lord!' Mrs Fletcher lifted her face to the ceiling and cried: 'Will this bickering never cease?'

Mr Fletcher, pressing his hand on Laura's shoulder, whispered: 'Come on, Lory. Don't get your mother started. We can knock these few things off in a brace of shakes.' Laura, calmed but sulky, followed him to the kitchen.

After tea, the household's turbulence died down. Mrs Fletcher sank into her chair, saying: 'This is the first time I've been off my feet today.' The cat came on to her lap. She read right through the *Daily Express* and the *Camperlea Evening Herald*. When she did not understand something, she read it aloud and Laura or Tom would say: 'It's meant to be funny, Mummy.'

Tom sat with his homework at one side of the table. Mr Fletcher sat at the other mending an old clock he had picked up in an auction room. The house was full of derelict objects he had picked up in auction rooms. The clock stood on the table, its back open, its entrails placed before him in orderly fashion, and picking up this piece or that he would murmur: 'That's the one. That's the chap we want.'

Laura read her holiday book, *Little Dorrit*. The television set, which could not get BBC 2, was never switched on until homework had been completed and books put away. It stayed on until around 10 o'clock, when Mrs Fletcher would get the supper milk.

She felt then that all were safely gathered in. With no pressures upon her, her mind's perpetually menacing whorl of fears and fancies slowed and grew lethargic. She, and her family with her, enjoyed as much tranquillity as they were ever likely to know.

On Thursday Mrs Fletcher said: 'Your father will go down to the bus stop with you and help carry your bags.'

Tom's brows rose in indignation: 'Aren't we having a taxi?'

Mr Fletcher jollied him: 'You don't need a taxi just to get to the pier.' Beaming, as he always did when he had presents for them, he produced two large nut milk bars, one for each, and put an end to controversy by lifting the suitcase. He handed the zipper bag to Tom and said: 'If we don't hurry, you'll miss the boat.'

Torn between anxiety and the relief of getting rid of them, Mrs Fletcher followed her children to the front gate with last minute warnings.

'All right. All right,' said Laura. 'We won't speak to any strange men, will we, Tom?'

Tom laughed in a near-hysteria of excitement and they both chased after their father who had set out at a brisk pace. Swinging on his arm, Laura said: 'Believe it or not, we're on our way.'

The three gave themselves up to conspiratorial laughter. As always when they had their father alone, Tom and Laura felt release and delight. Mr Fletcher's atmosphere was a holiday atmosphere, good-natured and gay. In early days they had seen him as a magical person who, by making passes in the air, could cause chocolate to be found in the living-room ornaments. When he used to take them for walks, there had been almost nothing they could not persuade him to do.

Laura, who pitied him and saw him helplessly trapped within her mother's agitated vortex, often dreamt of rescuing him and having him for herself; but he did not complain. He treated his secondary position in the house as a joke and with his children, played at being a child himself.

Laura said: 'Oh, Daddy, I wish you were coming with us.'

'I wish I were, too.'

'Couldn't you?'

'Hardly. Someone's got to look after your mother.'

Although she controlled everything, although she said 'I have to take every responsibility,' it was true that someone had to look after her. She felt too much; lived with too much difficulty; met every situation with nervous dread. Someone had to help her bear her ineptitude for life.

Laura feared she might be trapped by pity and like a warning of what might be, Miss Everest appeared, pushing the bath-chair down Rowantree Avenue.

Miss Vi Everest worked in the Public Health Department and in her luncheon hour hurried home to take her invalid mother out for an airing. Miss Everest was acclaimed by all as a good daughter, a daughter who had given her whole youth to looking after her mother. Seeing Mr Fletcher, Miss Everest came pelting the wheel-chair towards them, all her terrible teeth on view. Laura whispered to her father 'Say we're in a hurry' but it was too late.

Mr Fletcher was already calling out in welcome. 'Ah, the Everest girls!'

Though Mrs Everest was over eighty and Miss Everest

not yet sixty, they seemed the same age, and each was exactly like the other. People said both had been beautiful in youth and they were still beautiful in a macabre way. They looked like film stars of the old days, dead but embalmed; their red hair, skin of unearthly whiteness and lips like plum jam, all preserved intact. Long nylon lashes swept about their faded eyes.

Laura when a child had been frightened of these two identical faces. She was still frightened of them.

'Commander! Oh, Commander!' called Miss Everest: 'You'd never guess what my mamma said! She said: "Here comes my favourite man!"'

Mr Fletcher played up to them. Once, when asked to guess Miss Everest's age, he had said 'Twenty-five'. Unfortunately that time Mrs Fletcher had been with him and irritated by his persiflage, she shouted: 'Twenty-five indeed! She'll never see the day!'

Mr Fletcher flirted by instinct and scarcely knew any other approach to the women of his acquaintance. Miss Everest, who was fluttered by the mere sight of him, went on with piercing eagerness: 'And what do you think she said the other day? She was looking out of the window and she said: "There goes the commander. He's the handsomest man in Rowantree Avenue".'

'Girls, girls! You'll turn my poor head.'

Mrs Everest, whom Mrs Fletcher called 'stiff', said reprovingly: 'I fear, Commander, we're no longer girls.'

Automatically Mr Fletcher replied: 'With that blooming complexion, you'll always be a girl to me.'

Tom and Laura were in an agony of impatience. As the badinage went on, Laura pulled at her father's sleeve and when he did not heed her, she said: 'Oh, Daddy, do stop this imbecile talk. We're going to miss the boat.'

The Everests were shocked. Seeing Laura as the ill-behaved daughter of an offensive mother, Mrs Everest gave a sour smile: 'Dear me, Commander, we don't want to get you into trouble.'

Tripping over his feet in an effort to please everyone, Mr Fletcher let himself be dragged away but he said: 'Poor old things! You know, Lory, one has to be kind to people.'

Laura and Tom felt chastened for a few minutes then Tom gave a shout of dismay and pointed to the bus speeding past the end of the road. They were too far from it to run for it and, no longer chastened, they felt their mother had good reason to treat their father as a simpleton. Laura asked herself did he deserve to be rescued? She used to imagine all the fun they would have if they lived alone together but she was beginning to feel now that her father was too young for her.

Mr Fletcher was under orders to buy pork chops and take them straight home for the midday meal but he was so contrite that he remained at the bus stop and consoled his children by forecasting a week of fine weather. 'If you miss the boat,' he said, 'there'll be another one.'

Tom said peevishly: 'But we told Mrs Button we'd be on *that* boat.'

As the next bus edged into sight, Laura said: 'Grief, it's crawling.'

Mr Fletcher cheerfully said: 'It'll get you there all right.'

Knowing he would be in trouble enough when he arrived home late with the pork chops, Tom and Laura boarded the bus with no more than 'Good-bye'.

The bus meandered through the long main street where changes had taken place during the last five years. Shops that had not altered in half a century were being rebuilt, or given a modern polish, not for the sake of the North

Camperlea residents but to tempt the newcomers, the factory workers at Salthouse, who were reputed to 'have so much money they don't know what to do with it'. Though at street level there was redecorating and buying up of neighbours and opening of self-service stores that dazzled the eyes with light, the upper storeys were still the old house-tops of dark brick corbelled with painted stone.

That was Camperlea, Laura thought. Even when they reached South Camperlea and came into a region of turreted houses massed about with firs and evergreens, there was still the wine dark brick with the rendered parts painted the colour of custard. But in sight of the front where the sky broadened and the light seemed to grow lighter, the streets widened and there were plain, white-painted houses and elegant shops. Everything seemed to open up and reflect the windy brightness of the sea.

'Why can't we live here?' Laura grumbled, knowing the answer as well as anyone. Tom, relaxed in his seat, shrugged with philosophical calm and said: 'Can't afford it.'

If anything happened in Camperlea, it happened in South Camperlea. South Camperlea had developed before the war when the Navy set up an experimental sea-plane base. Mr Fletcher often spoke of the rollicking days when the hotels were full of officers, and smart bars and clubs and tea-rooms had started up along the front. The Town Council, thinking the town all set to rival Southsea, constructed a promenade and laid out the Flamingo Lake area of large houses. Camperlea's first ever block of flats was built at that time. Plans had been in hand to construct a new pier, but the glory did not last long enough. The Navy lost interest in sea-planes. The base was dismantled and all that remained of it was the hangar on Salthouse

Creek. Tom and Laura, hearing of this splendid past, were the more discontented that their native town was not only not what it might be, but not even what it had been.

As the bus ran along the front, they could see other relics of the sea-plane days for the winter tides, shifting the shingle, had disclosed stubs of rotting iron, scraps of barbed railings and rusty objects whose use no one in Camperlea now knew. They were contemptuous of this shore where the shingle was cruel to the feet. Why anyone came here on holiday they did not know. To them the holiday place was the Island where in childhood they had seen sand and rocks for the first time.

The pier was not a real pier. It was a wooden outbuilding off the shore big enough to hold a concert hall and round-abouts, bumper cars and booths with things you shot at. It stood near the corner where the sea ran inland to fill the big tidal basin of Salthouse Creek. In the distance, beyond the flat grey Salthouse shore and muddy muddle of creeks and marshy islands, could be seen the giant crane in Portsmouth dockyard.

'It's there,' Tom screamed when he saw the boat.

'In a hurry, eh?' said the ticket collector as they dragged their luggage in panic over the long flexing boards to the gangway.

'We thought we would miss it,' Laura explained.

'Miss it! This is the three-thirty. You've got more'n an hour before we go.'

Nearing the Island, Tom said: 'Do you think Mrs Button's been waiting all this time?' They were worried in case she had given up and gone.

Mrs Button had written to Mrs Fletcher: 'When I got that letter from your Laura I was that surprised. The children can come, and welcome, but with my legs they'll

26

have to do for themselves. I hope they'll remember me but I can't say I'm likely to remember them.'

'The old bitch!' said Mrs Fletcher, tossing the letter aside. There had been so much trouble over the trip that she could face no more. She did not speak of the letter to Laura and Tom but she drew two five-pound notes from her post office account and sent them to Mrs Button as 'a little something' towards the children's keep. Mrs Button's acknowledgement was conciliatory. She was, she said, looking forward to seeing the children again, especially Miss Laura who must be quite the young lady now. They would have 'all the home comforts' for her son Cyril did not stint his poor old mum. He now owned three garages but was as saucy as ever, she said.

The town, to which the boat was drawn as neatly as a toy pulled by string, climbed up the side of a hill. It was a climb of grey buildings with a steeple or two rising out of the muffling tree-tops. On either side of the pier – a real pier, this – there was a sandy shore.

Laura said: 'On the other side of the Island the sand is all colours.'

'How do you know?'

'I saw a glass lighthouse once, full of sand, all colours, in stripes.'

'We must get some of that,' said Tom.

No one at the end of the pier looked like Mrs Button. When everyone had been met by someone, there was no one left and Tom said fearfully: 'She hasn't come.'

'She didn't promise to come.' Laura realized they had expected her only from a habit of dependence: but this was freedom. They must look after themselves. 'Don't worry,' she said, 'we've only to find the right bus.' She noted with satisfaction that Tom, usually resentful of her

27

seniority, was happy to follow her now; still, she was not as confident as she sounded. She was reminded of all the warning that Mrs Fletcher – herself brought up by reserved, suspicious parents – had put out about the inhospitable world. Supposing they could not find Mrs Button! Supposing she had not come because she did not want them!

Relieved of responsibility, Tom was delighted by the half-size train and the length of the pier and the hovercraft that they saw skimming the water on its way to Southsea. Ryde looked friendly but they were not staying in Ryde. The bus took them to the hinterland – unknown but familiar, for it was only a piece of downland cut off from their own south downs – where there was hardly a house to be seen. They were still travelling when evening fell. But there was one comfort: the bus conductor knew Mrs Button's cottage and when it was nearly dark, he stopped the bus and said: 'Here you are!'

Laura and Tom were put down in open country over which loomed a lemony sunset streaked by strands of grey. There seemed to be a village in the distance but the only building nearby was a shabby little house with a fenced-in piece of scrub. 'I don't call that a cottage,' said Laura who had seen pictures of thatched cottages, 'but there's a light inside.' Their sense of adventure at nadir, they crossed the road and knocked on the door.

'So you found your way! I was beginning to wonder.' Mrs Button took them into the room and looked them over. Laura, 'quite the young lady', was expectant of attention, but Mrs Button summed her up with a glance then gazed at Tom.

'Well, young man, you've changed, you 'ave. You used to be a shrimp: always ailing. What a difference! You

28

weren't behind the door when looks were handed out, were you?'

Tom smiled his most winning smile and Mrs Button, patting his head, said: 'You want your tea, don't you?'

The room was very hot. It was a small room but Mrs Button had managed to fit into it a table and chairs, a three-piece suite, a cocktail cabinet and a television set. Everything was new except the gas fire that purred and gave out a homely, gassy smell. Mrs Button herself looked new: had they met her outside they would never have guessed she was Mrs Button. Her hair was auburn and she wore some remarkable glasses set with *diamanté*. Her red jumper-suit matched the red three-piece suite and her teeth, once brown and broken, were as white and even as her three-strand pearl necklace. She brought in two plates of ham and tomatoes, poured out some strong tea and said to Tom: 'Tuck in. There's the boy.' She sat on the sofa and smoked a cigarette while Laura and Tom, tucking in, described their journey in a riotous way.

Mrs Button let them talk themselves out then she stubbed her cigarette in a saucer. 'You got here. That's the main thing.' She looked at her watch and stood up. 'You can clear away. Now's about the time I go out to meet my friend. See you later, alligator.'

Surprised, Laura asked: 'But what will we do?'

'*Do?* You can work the set, can't you? It gets all stations.' Mrs Button put on her coat and was gone.

The television set was the most splendid Tom and Laura had seen. Settled on the sofa, they considered their situation. Ham for tea. No homework. A set that got all stations. This, they decided, was the life. But, strangely, it grew wearisome after a while. Ten o'clock passed and they discovered that the late night programmes could be ponderous stuff. They almost wished their mother were there to order them to bed. They were listening wearily to the weather report when Mrs Button banged open the front door and stumbled into the room. She looked in bewilderment at her guests then remembered who they were. 'You not in bed?'

Laura explained: 'We don't know where to go.'

'No more you don't. I suppose you want a cuppa.'

'No, thank you.'

'Well, I do.' Mrs Button was gone again and Tom, beyond caring, drew up his legs, shut his eyes and went to sleep.

When Mrs Button came back with her cup, Laura politely said: 'Please, Mrs Button, could you show us where we go to bed.'

'Hey, hey, don't you push me around,' said Mrs Button. 'I'm having my tea. Besides, young Tom here has to stretch out on the settee.' She lit a cigarette and when tea and cigarette were finished, said: 'Now I don't mind showing you up.' As she went ahead up the stairs a spiritous, fruity smell was wafted back to Laura and Laura thought: 'This is Experience.'

'You've got the Vanitory Suite,' Mrs Button said, leading Laura into the small front bedroom. She opened a cupboard to display not only wardrobe and shelves but a washhand-basin surrounded by pink plastic shelving and overhung by a neon-lit mirror. Laura was astounded.

'Like it?'

'Beyond dreams, Mrs Button.'

'My Cyril knocked it up. And I can tell you something: that mattress is a Slumberland. I bet you sleep like a top.'

Laura slept until nine o'clock and even then there was no one to harry her out of bed. She was stirred by the sound of Tom's voice coming up through the floorboards. He was at breakfast and lavishing his charm upon Mrs Button. Laura hastened to join them. Tom was eating bread, butter and marmalade.

Mrs Button was on the sofa. 'Help yourself,' she said to Laura.

'Aren't you having anything?' Laura asked with mature courtesy.

Mrs Button shook her head: 'Never was one for breakfast.'

She was richly clad in a housecoat of quilted nylon, tomato coloured and trimmed with gold, but she looked more like the Mrs Button they had known years ago. Before they had finished breakfast, she pointedly asked: 'And where are you two off to?'

'We want to go to the sea,' Tom said.

'The sea's just down the road.'

It was a brilliant, chilly day. Laura and Tom walked for two hours before they came to the edge of the land. Through a break in the cliff the wind struck them and they saw the sea glittering and crashing in upon a rocky shore. They had planned to bathe but when they tested it with their feet, they found the water as cold as winter. Anyway, they had no time to bathe. They would have to start back if they were to get their midday meal, which they regarded as the main meal of the day. They reached Mrs Button's house in good time but no one answered the bell. They tried the door: it would not open. All the windows were shut.

They soon learnt what was expected of them. They were to be out all day but in the evening there would be ham for tea. After tea they watched television while Mrs Button went to see her friend.

They adapted easily to this life. Mr Fletcher had given them a pound each and dividing their money so it would last the week, they fed at midday on chips if they could find a fish and chip shop, or hamburgers if they found a Wimpey bar. Mrs Fletcher's régime provided physical order and mental uncertainty. In Mrs Button's world this was reversed so Tom and Laura felt an exhilarating sense of self-reliance. And there were unexpected gifts. On Saturday night they were given hot shepherd's pie.

It was a wet evening. Tom and Laura had caught the bus and returned early, fearful of finding the house shut against them. Instead, the door opened. The room was warm and the gassy smell seemed to them the smell of home. While they were eating the pie, Tom said: 'Mrs Button, you're a smashing cook.'

Mrs Button, on the sofa as usual, said wryly: 'I always could cook, if I had anything *to* cook.' She lit a cigarette, smoked avidly for some minutes then said to Laura: 'Your mum wasn't much of a cook.'

'She says she's got too much to do.'

'She was a funny one.'

Laura was startled: 'How "funny"?'

'Oh, there was always something wrong. You never knew where you were with her.'

Laura and Tom exchanged glances, at a loss. They had remembered Mrs Button as eager to serve, agreeing with everything their mother said; but all the time, it seemed, she had been watching Mrs Fletcher with unfriendly eyes. Laura grew red and looked down at her plate. If she chose to criticize her mother, that was one thing: she would not condone Mrs Button's criticism.

'I often said to my Cyril: "She's got the doolallies, she has".'

Remembering all that her mother had given to Mrs Button – Mrs Fletcher was charitable by nature – Laura was roused to say: 'I don't know what you mean.'

'Oh, don't you!' Mrs Button spoke coolly. 'Well, you ought to, seeing as how you live with her. Rather you than me, though. Often when I looked at your dad I'd think "You poor old soul, I wouldn't be in your shoes, that I wouldn't".'

Tom, his plate emptied, stared at Mrs Button, his lips parted, a puzzled frown between his fine dark brows. Laura kept her head hanging. A guest, one who had just eaten Mrs Button's shepherd's pie, was not in a position to say much.

'Not that she didn't have her share. It's no joke with a man around all day. Your dad should have got himself a job.'

'He did have a job. He had to give it up. He had bronchitis.'

'Bronchitis! That's nothing. He could have got a nice little inside job. Camperlea's no good to anyone. If he'd gone to Portsmouth or Bournemouth, he'd have found a lot of nice little inside jobs. But there, she asked for it, marrying an old chap like him.'

Laura could not contain herself: 'Everybody loves Daddy.'

'Oh yes, he was affable enough. Always the gent. Never put you down. Don't think I'm knocking him but he needed a bit of push. He always seemed hoggers to me.' She stubbed out her cigarette and rose; 'I can tell you, it wasn't all honey working in that house. Well, I'll say ta-ta for the present. Clear the table before you go to kip.'

Having spoken her mind, Mrs Button went off to see her friend and Tom said: 'What did she mean –"hoggers"?'

'I don't know.'

Serious and concerned, Tom reflected before saying: 'I think she was being rude.'

'I'm not sure.'

'Why aren't you sure?'

'She didn't seem to think we'd mind.'

Subdued, they turned on the television set and consoled themselves with 'Z Cars'.

What Laura had promised, the Island gave. They saw palms and landfalls, chines and curiosities of nature; but they did not find the place with the coloured sands. They twice spoke of it to Mrs Button and she promised to ask in the village. On their last morning she said: 'I found out what they call that place you've been keeping on about. It's near Freshwater. If you get the bus, you've only got to ask the conductor.'

Expert now on Island travel, they took the bus to Freshwater and inquired the whereabouts of the fabled shore. The conductor said: 'You stay put. I'll tell you when you get there.' He was the thing Tom loved most in the world; a funny man. He ogled Laura until she was pink with self-consciousness and he made faces at Tom. When Tom asked where the bus was going, he sang 'Tot – Tot – Tot – lovely little Totland Bay'. Tom watched him entranced. The conductor winked at him and asked: 'Got a sack with you?'

Tom was all round-eyed innocence: 'What for?'

'To put the sand in, a-course. Come on now, nipper. Down the lane and it's straight ahead. You'll find all the sand you want.'

34

'*Coloured* sand?'

'Ever seen any sand that wasn't coloured? You got a bottle, 'ev'n't you?'

'No.'

'Better get a bottle. You'll want to take some home.'

Laura had walked off without a word and Tom, running after her, shouted: 'We've got to get a bottle.'

Following a track that ran below the edge of the downs, Tom talked about the conductor: 'Wasn't he super?'

'He was showing off.'

'Still, he was funny.'

'Not very.' Though tipsy with the conductor's admiration, Laura felt a need to decry her admirer.

As the path dropped, they could see the chalk cliffs as they curved to the headland. The sea, more silver than blue, lay idle about the Needles that stood in shadow, dark against the water, startling, a portent in nature.

Tom, in a state of excitement sped down the path shouting 'Beachy Head, Selsey Bill, St Catherine's Point, the Ne-e-e-d-les' while Laura, walking after with an exterior dignity, was moved by the sight of the formidable rocks that seemed to be allied with her own secret elation. She thought; if only Vicky and Gilda had been there to see the conductor goggling at her. But the thought sobered her. If Vicky had been there, the admiration would have been for Vicky.

At the end of the path, on the cliff-top, there was a chalet that sold glass shapes filled with sand. Tom and Laura had almost come to the end of their pocket money. They could, if they decided not to eat, buy a small glass tube in which to collect sand themselves. As they gazed and considered, Tom said: 'If we bought a bottle of pop, we'd have the bottle and the pop as well.'

'Scorchy idea,' Laura had to admit and they chose a Coca-Cola bottle as the one most worthy of permanent show over the Fletcher fireplace.

Running down the sea-bleached stairway to the shore, they came at last into the little sandstone bay where the sand was blotched rose-pink, rose-brown, yellow, slate-blue and violet-grey. Protectively held within the long arm of chalk, it was shielded from wind so even the sea came quietly in and out. Tom was disappointed. He had expected a much more violent collection of colours but Laura pointed out a boss of yellow, rich as Solomon's gold, and he became excited again: the yellow rock was almost inaccessible. He said: 'I bet I can climb up there.'

When they had emptied the bottle, drinking turn by turn, they washed it in the sea and set out over the fallen sandstone. They had decided to put the darkest sand at the bottom and work up through layers of brown, grey and pink to end with the golden yellow. Laura had a nail-file, Tom a pen-knife, and, squatting down, they scraped a handful from the purple rock.

'Now!' said Tom in a business-like way, holding out the bottle: 'Here's the bottom layer.' Laura poured carefully then gave a cry of disappointment. Instead of lying neatly where it was intended to lie, the sand caught itself on the moisture and blurred the whole of the inside glass.

Realizing their mistake, Tom laughed and sent the bottle flying out to sea.

Laura, angry because she had not foreseen what would happen, said: 'You grotty ass. There's thrippence on the bottle.'

'There *isn't*.'

'There *is*.'

'Oh well!' Tom shrugged but he knew that in their penurious state threepence was threepence.

With nothing but their bus fare back to the cottage, they started to walk to Totland Bay. They skirted families that, beguiled by the gentle day, had brought sandwiches and bananas and Thermos flasks full of tea. One small boy, working on a bucket-shaped castle, was too intent to eat. When his mother called, 'Come on, Terry, they're your favourite – roast beef sandwiches,' the Fletchers scarcely knew which roused in them more response; the creative activity they had outgrown or the food they had to pass, too polite to look closely, too hungry to look away.

Tom said, 'We'll be home for Sunday,' and they thought longingly of the Sunday meal of roast beef, Yorkshire pudding, roast potatoes and cabbage, which was the meal of the week.

They took off their shoes and let the water flood like ice over their bare feet while they walked on the myriad little red pebbles that formed a band between sea and shore. Out of a complex of emotions, Laura said: 'I don't want to go home.'

'Oh? Why not?'

'She never stops.'

'Well, neither do you.' Out of loyalty to his mother, Tom ran on towards a headland while Laura, trailing after, remembered, or remembered having heard about, when she was taken to the Selbys and told they liked her so much, they had invited her to stay there all day. She had only been four but she could remember that she was especially kind to Mr and Mrs Selby. She had danced and recited all the verses her father had taught her. She was there a long time and when the visit went on and on, she

37

began to ask for her mother and to feel her protracted stay puzzling and in some way disturbing. Late at night, or so it seemed, Mr Selby had walked her home and her own door had been opened by a woman she had never seen before. Whatever else she imagined, the strangeness of that strange woman returned to her with the impact of remembered reality. Then her father came running downstairs.

'I'll take her up.' He held her hand, reassuring her with his jolly manner: 'We have a surprise for you. A wonderful surprise.'

She had naturally thought it was a present for her, because everything had been for her in those days. She was, as she was often told, Mummy's 'pet lamb', Mummy's adored and fussed over baby. She had thought she was the only baby but when she went into the bedroom there was her mother in bed holding another baby.

'Look,' said Mr Fletcher as though the baby were a box of chocolates. 'Isn't he nice? A darling little brother for Laura.'

Laura stared at the horrible small dark face inside the shawl and said: 'I don't want it.'

Her father and mother and the strange woman all laughed at this but Laura was aghast at the deception that had been practised on her. She saw – probably a long time after – that the visit to the Selbys had been arranged so this creature could be brought in behind her back.

Laura had been dropped after that. The new baby, as Mrs Button said, was always ailing. A time of stress for Mrs Fletcher was for Laura a time of rejection. Laura seemed to hear like a panic cry from the past: 'Can't you get out of my way, Laura! Haven't I enough to worry about without being plagued by you?' Those words may have been sensed rather than heard. Though she remembered so clearly her first sight of the baby, she could remember very little after that. Whatever happened, Laura ceased to be pretty and charming and clever, and became instead a skinny little rat of a thing, unco-operative and given to boasting.

'She's stupid,' Laura said aloud. 'That's what she is: stupid!' and when she climbed over the litter of rocks and found Tom sitting on the other side, she said in a mischievous way: 'I tried to murder you once.'

Tom's eyes opened. Though startled, he appeared unconcerned: 'Oh? When?'

'When you were a baby. Mummy was carrying you downstairs. I put something on the stairs and she fell and nearly went to the bottom.'

Tom frowned, not really believing her: 'What did you put on the stairs?'

'A Thermos flask. She had to keep giving you special food and she used it to keep the food warm. She told me to take it down. I left it on the stairs and she put her foot on it and it slipped. You almost went over the banister. You must have heard about it.'

'No.'

Laura did not believe him but let it pass: 'She grabbed the banister and held on to your clothes. She saved you. It was clever of her, really. She used to say she could have killed me but I looked so frightened, she didn't say anything much.'

'But you didn't do it on purpose.' Tom, not liking the story, was reassuring himself, but Laura laughed and said: 'Perhaps I did. I don't remember.'

'But you couldn't. You couldn't have meant . . .'

Warned by the rise of his voice, Laura cut him short:

'Don't be silly. It was years ago. It may not have happened at all. Perhaps I invented it.'

They were a long way along the shore now. The tide was coming in. To get round the next headland they had to wade up to their knees and after all the effort, they found themselves in a desolate, rock-strewn bay from which there was no outlet. Already the water was too deep to let them wade back.

'We'll have to climb up the cliff,' Laura said.

'Bet you can't.'

'Bet I can. It's easy.'

The soft cliff stone had given lodgement to bushes and clumps of greenery. The way up seemed easy at first but half-way they came upon an earth terrace, quite flat, where there were trees and scraps of fencing and a perfect circle of strange blue clay. The cliff above was sheer without bush or crevice.

Looking down and seeing how quickly the tide had covered the rocks, Laura said with the steady practicability of fear: 'We've got to get up somehow.'

They pushed through the trees until they reached the base of the upper cliff and came upon the remnants of steps that had been beaten almost flat by the winter seas. Keeping his shoulder against the cliff face, Tom went up too quickly to fall. Laura tried to do the same thing but feeling her foothold crumbling beneath her, thinking the earth rock wall was crumbling above, she stopped and whimpered: 'I can't.' Tom was too far away to hear her and she had not intended to be heard. Swallowing her terror, she forced herself on.

Tom, looking down from the top, said in awe: 'It's someone's garden.'

They had expected to find the same common land they

had left at Alum Bay. Instead there was a levelled lawn with a table and a group of pretty ironwork chairs gazing seawards towards the mainland. The lawn, that ran back to an impressive house, was immense, the grass blades as small and fine as pine needles. On either side, behind trees, there was a wall and at the cliff edge the wall gave way to a fan of spikes which curved downwards to keep out intruders. Tom and Laura had come by the only back route to the house and unless they chose to climb down again, they would have to cross the lawn in full view of the windows. Tom, who had tackled the cliff bravely, now hung back. Laura, who had been fearful on the cliff, went forward without a thought. As they drew near the house, Tom whispered in alarm: 'There's a lady. There's a lady.

'Shut up. It's not our fault. We'll explain.'

The lady was sitting just inside an open french window. They hoped they might get past unseen. They kept in to the side, moving cautiously, intending to skirt the house, but the woman in the doorway had been watching them all the time. When they were near enough, she lifted a hand and beckoned them to approach. They came to a stop. Tom said: 'Let's bolt.'

Shocked, Laura said: 'She can't hurt us.'

'She's weird,' he whispered.

The woman's dress, of crimson satin, revealed her vast shoulders and arms but covered her feet. Her neck was held by an upstanding collar of pearls: diamonds gleamed and flashed on her bosom and about her hands and arms. Laura had seen the same sort of dress in pictures in the libraries. Queen Mary had dressed in this way and for all Laura and Tom knew, it might still be the dress of the very rich. The finery did not disconcert them but they were troubled by the woman's size and some inexplicable oddness of form that at this distance made them doubt if she belonged to the human race. She looked like a fairy-tale giant.

'Come a little closer. Let me take a look at you.' Though deep-voiced, the lady sounded amiable and they moved a few steps nearer the centre of the lawn. 'Come on,' she encouraged them, 'I won't hurt you.'

Foot dragging, ready to run if need be, they made their way to the door. The lady, enthroned at the top of the steps, her skirts spread around her, one elbow on a table, smiled at their unease. They could see she had been drinking from a tumbler and smoking a cigar. The cigar, a very large one, was burning itself out on the edge of an ash-tray and the lady let it burn. Her eyes, yellowish-blue, bulging and bloodshot, were fixed on Tom and Tom, susceptible as ever, smiled and went ahead of Laura.

'Come on. Come on,' said the lady and Tom mounted the steps and stood beside her. 'Now, young fellow m'lad,' she said, 'how did you get here?'

'We came up the cliff.'

'*Up* the cliff! Not many people come that way. You might have sunk into the blue slipper clay. A pity to lose a young fellow with eyes like yours. Still, you made it all right. No bones broken, eh?' The lady patted Tom's knees. Her fingers flashed and Laura, watching from the lawn, saw that her nail-varnish was silver. How odd they looked – the small, square silvery nails on those huge pink fingers! Still, Laura thought, this was a woman of liberal concepts. She smoked cigars while Laura's mother fussed and fidgeted over an occasional cigarette.

'What's your monaker?'

Tom laughed. 'Monaker?'

'Your name? Your name? Come on, young fellow, wake up.'

'Tom Fletcher. What's yours?'

'Mine? My name?' It was the lady who laughed now: 'Let's see! Mrs Toplady. That's it. Mrs Toplady. Not a bad name, eh? And where do you live? Not here on the Island?'

'No, we live in Camperlea. We're here on holiday, all by ourselves.'

'All by yourselves, are you?' Mrs Toplady made an appreciative noise and bent down to observe Tom more closely. 'Well, you are a handsome boy and no mistake.'

Laura, not given a chance to show where she had scratched her arm or torn her stocking, began to feel she had had enough of Tom's looks. Her Aunt Florrie, the spirited member of her mother's family, who had gone to Canada and married someone with money, had made the same sort of fuss of Tom when she saw him first. 'Tom's the one all right,' she said. When Mrs Fletcher protested that Laura was not bad looking, Florrie said casually: 'No, not bad. But it's hard on a girl when it's the boy that has the looks.'

Edging forward, observing but unobserved, Laura noted that Mrs Toplady's dress was much less grand at close quarters. It was stained and had burst open at the side. Though Mrs Toplady's curls were golden, her eyebrows were ginger and coarse ginger hair grew in her armpits. Her make-up was smudged and sticky and powder had settled in her pores so she seemed pock-marked like an orange. The worst thing was her mouth – a big, loose mouth on which she had drawn a tiny red mouth with peaked upper lip and under lip like a cherry. While Laura was observing Mrs Toplady, Mrs Toplady looked up and

43

caught her critical gaze. At once Laura dropped her eyes, abashed.

'Come up here, dear,' said Mrs Toplady and Laura went willingly up.

Mrs Toplady's manner changed with Laura. It became much more ladylike, a fact that Laura found flattering. 'You've got beautiful eyes, too,' she said: 'And such a slender figure!'

Giggling, Laura confided that the girls at school called her 'skinny'.

'Oh,' Mrs Toplady sighed, a languishing lady now, 'girls' schools are so bourgeois. I think you're perfect. If we had you in Paris, we'd make a cult of you.'

'A cult?' Laura was astounded.

'Indeed, yes. You're a *jolie-laide*. That's not to be sneezed at, I can tell you.'

A-tremble at this appreciation, Laura's excitement was such, she began wildly to boast: 'I can draw better than anyone else in the school. I'd like to be an artist except I'd like to write plays, too. I don't know what I shall do but I'm not going to do what my mother wants me to.'

'And what is that, dear?'

'Learn shorthand and go in an office.'

'Oh!' Mrs Toplady lifted a shocked hand. 'There are enough poor young things wasting their lives in offices. You've got to be different.'

'Oh, I will be.' Laura talked about her determination to go to London and though Mrs Toplady was sympathetic, her glance strayed towards Tom. Suddenly, in the very midst of Laura's plans for the future, Mrs Toplady burst out: 'Tom! Thomas. A perfect name for a perfect child!' She spoke so ardently, with such rich enunciation of the

44

word Thomas, that Tom blushed and Mrs Toplady, much amused, put an arm round his shoulder. Tom looked down and modestly smiled. He was, Laura noted, on his best behaviour and when on his best behaviour, he was as charming as a boy could be.

'Tell me, young fellow, what do *you* want to do when you grow up?'

Tom reflected before saying tentatively: 'I might be a rocket engineer. I'm not sure. It depends on what they pay.'

'Wouldn't you like to be a sailor? You'd make a fine sailor-boy.'

'No. I want to be rich.'

'Rich! How different from my young days! We wanted adventure. We never thought about being rich.'

'But you *are* rich.'

Mrs Toplady threw up her chin and laughed, then, pulling Tom to her, she pressed his head against her bosom. As she did this, Laura saw one of Mrs Toplady's breasts ride up out of the satin bodice; and it was not a real breast. It was made of pink plastic. Laura averted her gaze.

'Thomas!' Mrs Toplady spoke the name emotionally, giving it weight and darkness so Laura was reminded of plum pudding. Laura had never thought Thomas much of a name but Mrs Toplady seemed inspired by it. After she had repeated 'Thomas' several times, she said: 'It's like a very full burgundy.'

'Don't you think Vicky's a super name?' said Laura.

'Very nice. Is your name Vicky?'

'No, mine's draggy.'

'Draggy! Well, that's a nice name, too.'

Before Laura could make good this misunderstanding,

Mrs Toplady released Tom and noticing the pink plastic saucer, pushed it back as though it were a matter of no consequence. 'Would you like to see the Play Room?'

'What do you do there?' Tom asked.

'Play with the toys,' Mrs Toplady said.

Too old for toys, Laura and Tom would have preferred something to eat but hoping that, once inside the house, they would be offered food, they politely said 'Yes'.

Grunting with effort, Mrs Toplady got her vast backside out of the chair and rose to an impossible height. Towering over Laura and Tom, she looked with her yellow hair, highly coloured face and long red dress, like one of the ships' figureheads that Camperlea naval men put into their gardens. When she moved there was wafted from her the same plummy smell that came from Mrs Button. She took Tom's hand, and with Laura in the wake of her trailing crimson train, she walked awkwardly in red shoes with very high heels. They were the largest shoes Laura had ever seen and the heels sank into the grass. They went towards the trees at the side of the house.

'Isn't the Play Room inside the house?' Tom asked.

'No. It's over here.'

The afternoon was failing. The sun had dropped to the level of the cliff-top and the shadows, stretching and darkening, gave the trees a heavy, menacing look. The building hidden among the trees seemed menacing, too. The bricks were stained with green and the small, square windows were set so high no one, not even Mrs Toplady, was tall enough to see inside.

At the sight of it, Tom hung back and became fretful. 'What is it?' he asked, disliking it whatever it was. 'Is it a gym?'

Mrs Toplady laughed: 'A gym? I suppose you could

call it that. I told you – it's a Play Room. You'll see, when we get the door open.' The door was padlocked and dropping Tom's hand, Mrs Toplady began to feel inside her bodice. 'I have to keep it locked.'

'Why?' Laura asked. 'Are the toys valuable?'

'Not exactly valuable. They're rare and curious.'

Mrs Toplady had some difficulty with the padlock and the longer it took to open the door, the more reluctant Tom was to be shown anything. Laura could feel him straining back from the building but she held to him. Mrs Toplady had been so appreciative of both of them, they could not be rude to her.

The lock gave way at last. Pushing the door in, Mrs Toplady stood aside and motioned Laura and Tom to enter before her. Laura had to push Tom ahead and when they reached the threshold, he would go no farther. Standing on the step, they could see into an area large enough to be a gymnasium but much too crowded.

The late sunlight on the ceiling was reflected downwards so the room was half lit by a chrome twilight. Laura could make out a rocking-horse with something sticking up from its saddle. And there were dolls: life-sized doll children, naked, lying and standing in odd positions.

Tom, who had expected mechanical models of cars and aircraft, said with contempt: 'These aren't toys.'

'What are they, then?' Mrs Toplady sounded as though his opinion would amuse her.

'I wouldn't call them toys,' Laura said. Now that her eyes were becoming used to the dusk, she saw that the figures were too complete for dolls and she had never seen dolls in attitudes like these. Repelled yet curious, she tried to look closer but Tom stood in her way. He would not move and as she stepped forward, he twisted under her arm and stared at her, hysteria in his gaze. His voice was shrill and urgent as he shouted: 'They're not toys.'

'Yes, they are.' Mrs Toplady spoke persuasively, trying to pacify him: 'They're funny toys. They move. You can wind them up. If I put the light on you can see them properly.'

'I don't want to see them.' Tom was now in a panic and pushing past Mrs Toplady, he screamed: 'I won't see them . . . I won't . . . I won't . . .'

'Here!' Mrs Toplady's change of manner was abrupt and drastic. Bringing a hard and heavy hand down on Tom's scruff, she shook him violently, shouting: 'Stop that row. Shut up. Shut up, I tell you.' She gave his head a slap and threw him aside. Laura caught him as he fell and clinging together, they jostled out of Mrs Toplady's reach and looked for a way of escape.

'Wait,' Mrs Toplady commanded but they did not wait. As she locked the door, they threw themselves through the bushes and came out upon the peaceful lawn lit by the evening sun. Instinct took them to the other side of the house where they found, as they had expected, a path round to the front; but at the front they were not yet out of Mrs Toplady's demesne. A long drive stretched ahead of them through wooded grounds.

Tom called to his sister: 'Run, run.' He was near frenzy and as they ran, he started to sob with fear. Laura tried to comfort him: 'She'd never catch us. She'd trip over her skirt.'

'She was so big . . . like a monster. I don't think she was a lady. I think she was a man.'

'How could she be – dressed like that?'

The drive was glaucous with shadows when they

48

rounded the last curve and found a car coming towards them.

Tom gasped, 'Quick. Into the bushes,' but Laura slowed to a walk and pushed her hair from her face. She called Tom to heel: 'We've done nothing wrong.'

The man in the car was watching them keenly as he stopped in front of them and put down the window. They saw he was a chauffeur, young, with a leery, reddish face that detracted from his authoritative manner.

'You're trespassing,' he accused them. 'What are you doing here, anyway? Snooping around, I bet?'

His ordinariness gave them courage. Laura adopted a lofty, well-bred tone in which to tell him: 'We're not snooping. We were with the lady.'

'What lady?'

'Mrs Toplady.'

The man gave them a long quizzical look then decided to overlook their trespass: 'Hop it,' he said, 'and if you know what's good for you, you won't come back.'

He drove off and Laura, indignant at such treatment, turned on Tom: 'You were silly. A steaming nit.'

'How?'

'Making all that fuss. They were only dolls.'

'I didn't like them.'

'It would have been polite to look. She said they were rare and curious. We won't get another chance.'

'Who cares?'

They reached a gate. Outside there was a main road that probably was the road to Totland Bay. A hundred yards down, there was a bus stop. They had a long wait. Darkness fell, but they could wait with easy minds. In Camperlea it would be a different matter. Expecting them home, Mrs Fletcher would give them ten or fifteen minutes, then they would be in trouble. Here, if they did not return for tea, Mrs Button would probably go without a qualm to see her friend.

The holiday was almost over. They had known for a short time the simplicity of independence. Tomorrow they must face again the emotional confusion of home.

2

THE PLAY ROOM

A vision of Mrs Toplady, too gross to be real, persisted at the back of Laura's mind. It was there a long time, disturbing and equivocal, and was exorcised only when Laura remembered the word *Experience*.

She imagined she knew everything but had to admit there was more to life than knowledge. Experience was what she needed. The Play Room figures had been disquieting but they were actual; not something invented by Mrs Toplady to frighten her visitors. If they had let her wind up her dolls, what might they not have seen and learnt?

Mrs Toplady herself had been no ordinary woman. She was exceptionally perceptive, Laura thought. She had said, 'If we had you in Paris, we could make a cult of you.' Laura began to feel regrets. If she had explained how unsatisfactory life was in Camperlea, Mrs Toplady might have said, 'Why not come with me to Paris?' Laura saw herself in a new city where she was a different person and treated as a different person. A cult – whatever that implied. Instead, here she was back at Buckland House School where she was held to be a cross between a prodigy and a joke. She felt she was a prodigy but she had no proof of it. She might be only a joke, after all. The uncertainty confused her. She knew she was always saying the wrong thing; and was rude when she had everything to lose by being rude. The only person who had shown her sympathy was Vicky. The only teacher who attempted to understand her was Miss Lamb. One day Miss Lamb had asked her, 'Why do you behave so badly, Laura?' and Laura, overset, as she always was, by kindness, burst out, 'Oh, Miss Lamb, I'm so ugly.'

She wanted to be told, 'You're not at all ugly' but instead Miss Lamb made the conventional reply about looks not being everything. It was an incident that added to Laura's uncertainty, yet even the harsh judges of Buckland House had never said she was ugly. Once she had intercepted a note which was being passed under the desk and supposing it to be for her, she had opened it and read: 'Do you think Laura Fletcher is pretty?' The reply, three times underlined, was 'No'.

That had been comfort in a way. At least there was doubt about her looks. Her face was oval, her skin clear and viewed from the front, she was *almost* pretty. But her nose was too long, her chin too short, her arms and legs too thin, her head small and she had dark unbiddable hair. There had been that painful occasion when she spent her pocket money on a pair of black stockings. They were doing the Arachnid in Nature Class at that time and when she came in, Gilda Hooper had screamed out: 'Grief! One of the Phalangidae!'

Laura knew she had sad defects and nothing could overcome them. It seemed to her that if you were born with a nose too long and a chin too short people felt it was your own fault. Girls with faces as plain as porridge could congratulate themselves that their noses were short and their chins long. Cube-shaped girls were satisfied that no one would scream at them, 'One of the Phalangidae!'

Coming on top of all that, Vicky's remark about Bobby

Bonham had made Laura feel hopelessly condemned. But Mrs Toplady had looked on Laura with different eyes and Laura's defects were seen to be admirable. 'You're a *jolie-laide*,' Mrs Toplady had said and Laura need not worry about the prescripts of Buckland House. Her future, she felt, was in a wider world.

Everyone except the Head Girl returned for the summer term. Sarah Jackson had left to take A levels at the Technical College. The back-row pedants discussed who should succeed her but, with Sarah gone, Laura felt it scarcely mattered who was chosen. The only person worthy of the position was Vicky Logan and Vicky, always at the bottom of the class, would never be a candidate.

Waiting for the first lesson on the first day of term, Laura got out her sketch-book and drew a picture of Vicky with a circlet round her head and wrote underneath: 'And she was taken out of the bottom desk and crowned Head Girl because she was the most generous and most kind and most beautiful of all. Laura Fletcher, her handmaiden, bearing witness, said: "When all people rejected me, Victoria Logan lent me a handkerchief".'

Vicky was not in the room and might not be coming back. She was sixteen. Why should she stay here and sit in the bottom desk when the outside world would crown her for being nothing but herself.

Yet just as the lesson began, Vicky came in, breathless and apologetic. She was a tall girl: the front desk was too small for her but she squeezed on to the seat and shaking back her long ash-fair hair, gave Miss Lamb her serious attention.

Gilda Hooper was back, of course. Little hope that she would leave while Vicky remained at Buckland House. At the first tinkle of Break and Luncheon bells, Gilda was on her feet, taking possession of Vicky; and Vicky, sprawled across her desk, waited to be possessed. At luncheon hour Gilda would pull Vicky up and they would go to the basement dining-room where they sat at one of the small tables, whispering together. All winter during Break, Gilda would squeeze into Vicky's desk and the whispering would go on. Now the weather was warm enough, they would go out in the garden to whisper.

On the first day of term Gilda hurried to join Vicky as though they had been separated for an age. In fact, they had probably seen each other every day during the holiday. Laura could imagine them, arm in arm, walking along the Camperlea front where, so Gilda said, all the best-looking boys came out in search of them.

In the garden the more social girls would stay in groups on the lawn. Those who preferred the company of a Best Friend would stroll down the long path under the apple trees, heads bent together in intimate confabulation. Gilda usually took Vicky down to the bottom of the garden to talk, avoiding the rest as though they were in a nest of eavesdroppers.

Laura, whose attempt at best friendship with Valerie Whittam satisfied neither of them, had spent the previous summer going from group to group on the lawn, trying to entertain everyone as though she were the school jester. Well, she would do no more of that.

Standing alone against an apple tree, she watched Vicky and Gilda go by. Gilda was a strongly built girl with a round hairy, coarse-skinned face. In his petty-officer days, Mr Hooper had been stationed at Malta and had married a

Maltese. Mrs Hooper was said to have been the prettiest girl in Valletta but now she was a wrinkled, shrunken little woman who looked more like a grandmother than a mother. Gilda was sallow like her mother but she had the misfortune to look like her lumpish father. In spite of that, she was always telling the class that some boy or other was mad for her. No one, not even Sarah Jackson, questioned her claim. There was an odd smell about her that could be the smell of sex, and she was a girl who took what she wanted.

She had, for instance, taken the position of Vicky's Best Friend though she had no more right to it than Laura. Less, Laura now thought, for Vicky had lent her a handkerchief and surely the gesture had united them? The trouble was, as usual, Laura's diffidence. She had simply hoped Vicky would approach her again but Vicky was too indolent to approach anyone.

It had been opportunity lost. Standing under the apple tree, Laura began to see it as opportunity appropriated. Gilda, coming to the school soon after, had simply stolen Vicky: and Laura, believing herself dispossessed, began to wonder if she could break into this Vicky–Gilda combine. The very thought frightened her and had it come to her in the past she would not have considered it, for Gilda had a viper's tongue and used it like a viper. Now, though frightened, Laura was excited; though she was not excited enough to act, the thought remained with her all afternoon and at tea she was so silent, Mrs Fletcher said: 'What's the matter with this one? Not a complaint out of her.'

Waking at four in the morning, she asked herself: 'Why should that pig Gilda get away with it?' Laura decided to act and decision reached, she was able to sleep again.

A month passed before she found courage to intervene

but during that month she observed the relationship between Gilda and Vicky. One day when it was too wet for the garden, Gilda, pushing as usual into Vicky's desk, put on an air of mock sternness and said, 'Shove up, you!', speaking loudly so the whole class might know that Vicky was hers to command. To Laura it seemed that Vicky, smiling as ever, complied with tolerance rather than enthusiasm. Was the friendship anything more than a game to her? When they were together in the desk, Vicky would keep her head bowed so the curtains of her hair, falling shut, hid her face. Gilda, lying against her, would whisper into the silken hair persuasively, almost amorously it seemed. At times, when doing this, she would lose her seat in the uncomfortable little desk and almost slip to the floor. Then what a lot of noise and giggling! And once, ostentatiously, Gilda blamed Vicky and gave her several playful slaps.

Gilda was not one to share the bottom desk with just any girl. She wanted Vicky but she also wanted Vicky's lustre. Vicky was aureoled with romantic tragedy. Her brother had been thrown off his motor-bicycle and killed and her mother, ill with grief, had had to have Vicky at home to attend her. Because Mrs Logan was never really well again, the Logans went on winter holidays to places like Marrakesh and the Canary Islands. Vicky had been taken away from a boarding-school in Brighton and sent to Buckland House where no one worried about her absences. She missed so many weeks at school that, even here they could place her no higher than the bottom of the Upper School. This position, that would have been ignominious for another girl, simply marked Vicky as someone apart. She had the privileges of difference and took no part in the rivalries of school.

Laura had been a little girl when there was so much talk about Ronnie Logan's accident. People had said how shocking it was that the young man had been killed, while the motor-bicycle was unscratched. Then, two or three years after the accident, there had been all the fuss about Mr Logan's design for the Camperlea reading room.

People wrote to the *Camperlea Herald* to say the room was much too large. It was painted in impracticable colours and had a black ceiling which was described in the paper as 'unheard of'. The long sofa seats had no backs but were upholstered in shades of fuchsia and shocking pink. One wall was entirely of glass but all this glass looked on to nothing more than a corner of the park given over to a compost heap, a potting shed and a dozen wheel-barrows.

The letters filled two pages of the paper. In reply Mr Logan said that while Camperlea remained moribund within the limited, class-ridden concepts of the thirties, an artistic revolution had revivified the outside world. People wanted brilliance and colour: they wanted space and light. The reading room was designed to answer the demands of the modern world.

Still, nobody liked it except, of course, Laura. The regular readers – old-age pensioners and chronic invalids for the most part – disliked it more than anyone. They resented the brilliance of the seats and seemed to feel that the atmosphere called for a special breathing apparatus, the lung area of a higher species. Even after walls and seats had been made homely with grime, they sidled in suspiciously, condemning the room as too big, too brightly lit, too aesthetic for human use.

Mr and Mrs Fletcher, members of the Ratepayers' Association, disapproved the room without ever going to look at it. Laura said in exasperation: 'Mr Logan's been to London. I suppose he knows what he's talking about.'

This statement roused in Mrs Fletcher the most extreme indignation.

'Don't talk to me about the Logans.' She had heard all about them from Mrs Vosper. 'Logan's father was a builder who got a contract to build air-raid shelters and he used such rubbishy material, the shelters just collapsed. He was put in prison.'

'I suppose you think the reading room's going to collapse?' Laura contemptuously asked.

'I don't care if it does.'

Laura, intoxicated by this information about Vicky's grandfather, could see no limit to Vicky's allure. A brother killed, a mother prostrate, a father accused of wasting public money – and now a grandfather who went to prison! Had there ever been another girl so adorned by events?

Laura reached the moment of action one summer day when the blossom had fallen and the apples were forming on the trees. She had just seen Vicky slip out of Gilda's hold as though the weather were too hot for contact (which it was not) and then, throwing back her hair, gaze up through the apple trees as though there, somewhere above the branches with their leaves and tiny apples, there was something more desirable than the embrace of Gilda Hooper.

Laura's emotions rushed out in response. Her heart pounding, she ran to Vicky and said: 'What do you think!'

Turning her beautiful, mild gaze, Vicky smiled in inquiry. Laura hurried on: 'You know my brother and I went to the Island at Easter? Well, we saw something. Something fan-*tas*-tic.'

Gilda, a step behind Vicky, looked furious at this breach of their privacy. Given the chance, she would speak her mind but Vicky was encouraging Laura. Unfortunately Laura, choked by her own daring, could only repeat: 'Fantastic. Fantastic.'

Gilda crossly asked: 'What was fantastic?'

'What we saw.'

'Get on with it, then. What *did* you see?'

Laura swallowed deeply and having ingested her agitation, told of the meeting with Mrs Toplady. She wanted to spin out the story, reserve some of it for a possible other venture, but she talked too quickly and reached the Play Room before she knew where she was. She stopped abruptly.

Interested in spite of herself, Gilda urged her on: 'What happened then?'

'The door was locked. She had the key in her dress. It took her ages to get it open.'

'And what was inside?'

'You'd never guess.'

'Nothing much, I bet. A lot of old games, I suppose?'

'No, not games. Not anything you've ever seen.' Laura laughed and glanced about her with an air of containing her knowledge.

'You're being very mysterious,' Vicky said.

'We thought Mrs Toplady was weird.'

Laura paused and after an interval, Gilda demanded: 'Did you see anything or didn't you?'

'I've told you: we did. We didn't stay long . . . In fact, we bolted; still, we saw enough.'

'Well, then?'

Managing to protract her silence for one more minute, Laura was saved by the bell. 'Tell you another time,' she shouted and ran back to the school-house.

During French Conversation, Gilda sent a note under the desks. Brows were raised when it was seen that the addressee was Laura Fletcher but Laura received it as though a note from Gilda were an everyday affair.

'Write it down,' Gilda had written. Laura's reply was: '*Im*-possible.' Gilda's heavy eyebrows drew together. She stared round fiercely but Laura kept a lamb-like gaze upon Mademoiselle Contanseau.

In the cloakroom later, Gilda gripped Laura's arm and said: 'It was just one of your mock-ups.'

'It was not.' Aware of Vicky's amused attention, Laura postured before the cloakroom glass, saying: 'Mrs Toplady said I'd be a cult in Paris.'

Gilda moaned 'Grief!'

'She said I was a *jolie-laide*.'

'A *what*?'

'She meant that though I was ugly I was attractive.'

'Ger-reef!'

'She was right,' Vicky said. 'Laura *is* attractive in an odd way.'

Gilda groaned again. Vicky, her school-hat sitting like a halo on the back of her fair head, gave Laura a rapid flutter of an eyelid and Laura blushed with triumph. This more than made up for the Bobby Bonham remark.

'Come on,' Gilda tried to harry her, 'what did you see in this Play Room?'

'Haven't time now. Mummy wants me to do some shopping. I'll tell you in Break tomorrow.'

'You needn't bother. We don't care.' Gilda turned her back on Laura and Laura, drunk with Vicky's approval, sped off, giggling. Next day she was less assured. Gilda ignored her and kept Vicky out of her way. So far as they were concerned, Laura had ceased to exist.

It was a Friday. She had the whole week-end in which to wonder whether, being clever, she may not have been too clever.

On Monday morning it was raining and Gilda joined Vicky in her desk. Laura, pretending to examine a calendar on the fireplace shelf, stayed invitingly near, but Gilda and Vicky seemed unaware of her. Vicky was finishing an essay that should have been her week-end task. Laura, unable to leave them, watched Vicky form large, sketchy letters that from boredom grew larger and larger until the words at the bottom of the page were half an inch high. The page filled, Vicky glanced up and catching Laura's entranced gaze, smiled mischievously: 'Seen any good play rooms lately?'

Laura stepped eagerly forward and said in a low voice: 'I wanted to tell you but not here.'

Gilda frowned and asked: 'Why? What sort of things were they?'

'Can't you guess?'

Gilda and Vicky stared at Laura. Vicky's wide soft mouth fell open and for once she was not smiling. Her expression, intent and grave, suggested that in a world where she held most things lightly, Laura had touched on an aspect of life that she took seriously. She said: 'Could you come to tea on Saturday?'

'Yes, of course.'

'Come about three. We can talk in the garden where no one can hear us.'

'Thanks. I'd love to.'

Laura's elation lasted until she reached home then she felt alarm. She had not been invited for herself but for what she had to tell. And what had she to tell?

She could imagine Gilda's contempt when she learnt that the things in the Play Room were dolls. Only dolls? What a swindle! True they were life-sized dolls but they had been the silliest sort of dolly dolls. Apart from a few additions, they were as inane as shop-window dummies. Their attitudes were intended to startle but would they startle girls who knew as much as Vicky and Gilda?

Laura saw herself shamed. Vicky would be too kind to say much, but how Gilda would scoff!

When Laura was silent again at the tea-table, Mrs Fletcher said: 'I don't know what's come over this girl these days.' She would have questioned Laura sharply but her attention was diverted by her husband saying:

'Met an old ship today – Dinty Moore. I was surprised. He hasn't put on an ounce of weight. He said to me: "Fletcher, you'll have to cut down on bread, sugar and potatoes. You'll have to go on a diet".'

'Oh, did he!' said Mrs Fletcher. 'And what does he think you're going to eat, I'd like to know.'

'Oh, fish and eggs and cheese. He said I could have as much meat as I liked. And fruit.'

'Did he, indeed! We could all do with that diet; but who's going to pay for it? You don't know what a worry it is feeding four people on your small pension.'

Laura sighed. A conversation about money could last right through the meal. The most important day of the month was the day Mr Fletcher went to draw his pension. He always went on a Saturday morning and would return home beaming, feeling, for once, important in his rôle as provider. On that morning, Mrs Fletcher, too, would be in a good humour as though the money meant some special treat for them all. In fact, every penny of it was ear-marked for the necessities of life.

Laura could remember a morning when her father, plump, pink-faced, the bearer of sustenance, pulled out the notes and scattered them all over the living-room table. 'There you are,' he said. 'Do what you like with them.'

Laura and Tom, much smaller then, had screamed with delight, imagining he meant what he said. Tom shouted, 'Can we have them? Can we really have them?' and Mr Fletcher laughed, saying: 'Yes, you can have them if you like; but you'll have nothing to eat for the rest of the month.'

Even then the scattered notes had transported them with a sense of plenty. Tom asked: 'How much is there?'

Gathering the money up, Mrs Fletcher said: 'Nearly eighty pounds.'

'That's a lot,' Tom said.

'And there's a lot to be done with it.' Mrs Fletcher prided herself on being a good manager. 'And I need to be,' she often said. When she had all the notes in her hand, she sorted them into small bundles, saying: 'The rates, the water-rates, gas, electricity, income tax, school bills, clothing, housekeeping, the mortgage and extras. Now, you see the way I've divided the money up! I believe in putting away a little each month and when the bills come in, the money is ready. That's how we pay our way.'

The children were sobered. The festive scattering of banknotes had ended in a lesson in household management. The money had seemed such a lot of money – surely they could do more than just pay their way?

Now they knew that £80 a month was not a lot of money. Mr Fletcher sometimes said there was talk about giving the older naval pensioners a rise in pension so they might, in the end, get as much as Mr Hooper who by the great good fortune of being six years younger than Mr Fletcher not only got a grant of three thousand pounds but a pension of nearly a hundred pounds a month. When they first heard this, Laura and Tom protested 'It's not fair,' but Mr Fletcher was, as he always was, philosophical.

'That's what the world's like,' he said: 'Some people are luckier than others. I got the same pension as the others who retired when I did. I can't complain. And one day, perhaps, they'll give us a little more.' That day was talked about but it was, as Mrs Fletcher said, 'a long time coming'.

Vicky and Gilda had spread a rug on the lawn and were lying comatose in the early summer sun. The lawn ran all round the house, one of the Flamingo Lake colony of houses built by the late Mr Logan, the 'Old Logan' who had gone to prison. Laura arrived apprehensively, but she arrived. Curiosity, if nothing else, took her on Saturday to Flamingo Park. She had to see Vicky's house. Should her story fall short of expectation, she thought she could invent a few Play Room horrors. Vicky and Gilda might not believe her but they would not be disappointed.

Coming to the edge of the rug, she said 'Hello' and Vicky, lifting the arm that was across her eyes, said 'Oh!' as though she had forgotten her invitation to Laura. If she had, Gilda had not. She at once made it clear that not for nothing had Laura the privilege of their company. Even as Laura seated herself, Gilda said: 'Come on. Let's have it.'

'For grief's sake!' Vicky covered her eyes again. 'Let the girl get her breath.'

Laura said: 'The things were dolls, but not ordinary dolls.' She described what she had seen and, surprisingly, the truth was enough. Vicky sat upright. 'You don't mean it?'

Gilda's black, critical eyes seemed to spark. 'You can't be serious?'

'I am. I saw exactly what I told you.'

'Ger-reef.' Gilda threw her arms round Vicky who clung to her. They rocked together in ecstasy.

'And they were complete?' Gilda insisted: 'The boys, too?'

Vicky shushed her: 'Anyway, there are boy dolls like that in America.'

'Yes,' Gilda screamed, 'but these were big ones.'

'Do shut up,' Vicky said, laughing delightedly.

'But they were, weren't they?' Gilda turned on Laura: 'You said they were life-size.'

'Yes, but at art schools . . .'

'Art schools! Don't be a steaming nit. These weren't classical models?'

'No, nothing like. They were dolls.'

Gilda made her repeat her description of the dolls and their postures until Laura became bored and said: 'You've heard it all.'

Gilda bent close to Vicky and whispered, 'Let's make her tell it again' but Vicky, agreeing with Laura that enough was enough, shook her head.

'Wasn't it fan-*tas*-tic though?' Gilda said.

Vicky murmured 'Beyond dreams' and lay down again.

Laura, her ordeal over, glanced round the nurtured, flower-filled garden and said 'Super garden' though she thought she preferred the spacious simplicity of the garden belonging to Mrs Toplady. One bed was massed with geraniums, the pots showing above the soil, the colours violently fresh against the lawn's fresh green. The lawn roused her admiration.

'It's dwarf grass,' Gilda spoke proudly of the Logans' splendours.

'I think Mrs Toplady had dwarf grass,' Laura said, though Mrs Toplady's grass had not been as green as this. Nothing about Vicky had prepared Laura for the prosperity shown here. Money meant display in Camperlea and display was admired, but Vicky herself was not given to display. Everyone knew, of course, that she lived in Flamingo Park but it had been old Mr Logan's house and Laura had imagined the Logans living there merely as inheritors, indifferent to the conventions and rivalries of Camperlea's monied class. But what she saw here did not suggest indifference. The Logans spent their money so Camperlea could see the results.

Laura had always thought of Vicky's beauty as a marvel, its origin only in itself. Now, seeing her out of school uniform, her exquisite bosom held in a green silk shirt, her legs, long, creamy and flawless, stretched out of green linen shorts, Laura could see that a great deal of care had gone to the making of Vicky. She was a rich girl, a privileged girl, and Laura felt herself to be neither.

Yet Gilda, whose upbringing had probably been quite haphazard, was at home here and rather more in possession than Vicky. Turning and meeting Laura's appraising stare, Gilda said: 'We're going to the St Barnabas' Fête.'

'When?'

'Oh, not now. Later. It's a special occasion. They're having a barbecue and a dance.' Leaning against Vicky's hair, she said: 'I know who'll be there.'

She whispered a name and Vicky smiled: 'Maybe.'

'Of course he'll be there. We can go on the bike, can't we?'

'I suppose so. Mummy says she'd rather we didn't.'

'I bet she says it's not safe.'

'Yes, and not nice. She thinks girls shouldn't ride large motor-cycles.'

'How dim can you get!'

'She's had some shocks, you know.'

'Oh, I know,' Gilda sighed, rather less from sympathy than from impatience.

Vicky aware of Laura watching and listening, turned to her and said: 'Would you like to come with us?'

'To the dance?' Laura was in the regulation school skirt, which was two inches above the knee: 'I couldn't come in this,' she said: 'You need a mini for dancing.'

'A mini with your legs?' Gilda said. 'What would you look like?'

'Well, I wouldn't look like a grotty elephant.'

Unaware of Laura's skill at tea-table debate, Gilda could not speak for astonishment and Vicky, half shielded by her hair, smiled at Laura and winked.

Laura appealed to her: 'Would I look awful in a mini?'

'You'd look no worse than most girls.'

Laura, encouraged, said ardently: 'Vicky, don't you *long* to go to London?'

'I haven't thought about it.'

'But it's super, Vicky. Everyone's swinging. I mean not just young people, but old people like our mothers. And people are not always getting at you. There's this wonderful spirit of tolerance.'

'Someone's been leading you up the garden,' Gilda said.

'It's true. I've read it. I haven't just read it in *Vogue* and *Harper's*, I've read it in all sorts of places.' Laura swung her head round to look directly at Vicky: 'Vicky, don't you want to live there?'

Vicky, sprawling, her lips on her arm, yawned and said: 'I don't think I do. I'm all right here. Surely you wouldn't want to live alone?'

'Yes, I'd like to live alone. I'd rather live there than anywhere. You can earn a lot of money – you get about twelve pounds a week for working in a coffee bar where

70

it's fun all the time. And the men! Here they all look like bank clerks. In London they wear super clothes, all colours.'

Laura could not accept Vicky's uninterest. 'You can't stay here, Vicky. It's terribly slug. Your father said that Camperlea's stuck in the class-ridden concepts of the thirties.'

'Did he say that?' Vicky was amused.

Gilda, frowning over her companions like a jealous black poodle, said: 'This is all bloody silly. Camperlea's not bad. We often have pop groups on the pier. There's a pop group at St Barnabas.'

'Yes, but nobody screams or anything. They're all repressed.'

Vicky slid her glance sideways to look at Gilda and Gilda tittered. Laura, discouraged, dropped down on the rug and shutting her eyes, saw herself walking in night-time Soho through a street a-dazzle with lights, where nobody slept. There were discotheques and dance clubs and cafés and coffee bars and young men by the dozen: young men beyond dreams, with lean pliable bodies and hair curling on their shoulders, as beautiful as archangels, in clothes all colours. And she could imagine Vicky walking beside her! Everyone would look at them. *Everyone.*

As Laura raised herself to speak again, a voice called from the house: 'Tea's ready.'

Gilda jumped up. Vicky held out her arms and Gilda, laughing loudly, heaved and struggled and pulled her to her feet. Both standing, Gilda put her arm round Vicky's neck and murmured against her ear: 'Shall I iron your hair before we go?'

'Mummy keeps saying she wishes I'd leave it alone.'

'Grief, you don't want a wave, do you?'

'I suppose not.'

The woman who had called them in was standing in the hall: 'Your mum's got a bit of a head,' she said, 'so no shouting and laughing, mind.'

Vicky nodded meekly and they went into a room large and light coloured, with a surprising number of satin-covered chairs and sofas. Mrs Logan sat in an alcove formed by a big bow window and there, it seemed, life was lived. They were not to take tea round a dining-room table. The tea things were put all together on a trolley beside Mrs Logan. Though Laura was overwhelmed by this proof of elegance, she saw there was nothing to fear.

Mrs Logan could not frighten anyone. She had none of Vicky's beauty but her wan sweet little face had been coloured and decorated with an artistry that Laura found impressive. Catch Mrs Fletcher going to all that trouble!

Laura, when introduced, said with enthusiasm: 'Oh, Mrs Logan, what a super view!' This she could safely say for the view down to Flamingo Lake was described by estate agents as 'the most desirable view in South Camperlea'. In North Camperlea, of course, there were no views.

Mrs Logan was as enthusiastic as Laura. 'Oh, it's ever so nice,' she said. 'I do enjoy watching the kiddies with their boats.'

Young Logan (so Mrs Vosper said) had married beneath him. This meant that Old Logan, though a self-made man and one who had gone to prison, was richer than Mrs Logan's father who had been landlord of the Admiral Howe. So unpretentious was Mrs Logan that even after years in Flamingo Park she still had a trace of Camperlea accent.

'Sit down, dear, do,' she said, looking as though she were very pleased with Laura.

72

Gilda had already seated herself, landing heavily in the biggest armchair, while Vicky waited by her mother, intending to hand round plates and cups.

'How's my little girl?' Mrs Logan smiled up into Vicky's face: 'You know, darling, you should wear a sun-hat in the garden.'

Vicky smiled down indulgently: 'Shall I pour the tea, pet?'

'Yes, do.' Mrs Logan let herself sink back with a little sigh. 'I walked all the way to the Clematis and when I got there the cream horns had gone. Oh, I was disappointed. I said to the girl: "I've come from Flamingo Park especially."'

'Never mind, Pettikins, the cheese-cakes look lovely.'

'I don't know.' Sadly eyeing the cheese-cakes, Mrs Logan sighed again and looked at Laura: 'I do love a cream horn,' she said.

Laura was filled with wonder. The agitated revolt of her own home had seemed to her the natural condition of parents and children. Now, amazed, she observed Vicky's tender concern for her mother and Mrs Logan's tender response to Vicky. At the same time, knowing that Mrs Logan was a centre of tragedy, she wished she, too, could stand beside her and protect her from all unkindness.

Vicky was rallying her mother as one might rally a hurt child: 'They're super cheese-cakes. Beyond dreams.'

'Beyond dreams!' Now it was Mrs Logan who smiled indulgently and bending a little towards Laura, she said: 'What does it mean – "beyond dreams"? I never know.'

She spoke as though Laura were someone older and more authoritative than herself and Laura eagerly replied:

'I think it means "so super you couldn't even dream about it"'.

'Isn't she a clever girl?' Mrs Logan appealed to Vicky: 'As soon as I saw her, I said to myself: "Here's a clever girl."'

'She's the youngest in the Upper School,' Vicky said.

'And,' said Laura, 'I'm taking O levels this year.'

'Are you, now?' Mrs Logan nodded in appreciation then, after a few moments, repeated: 'Beyond dreams!' and consulted Laura again: 'That's what life should be, isn't it? Beyond dreams.'

Laura sensed a fault in this proposition and instead of replying, said: 'Oh, Mrs Logan, I do think you're super. You give me hope for my own old age.'

Mrs Logan laughed a long and happy laugh; and Vicky looked pleased.

During this conversation Gilda, looking remotely amused as though she could not take seriously any talk about Laura, gave herself to the food. Aware she was out of it, Mrs Logan turned to her and kindly asked: 'How is Gilda today?' Gilda, her fat cheeks full of cake, chewed and swallowed and sat upright, prepared to talk about herself.

Tea over, Vicky said: 'You know, pet, we're going to the St Barnabas' dance.'

'Oh, yes, of course.' Mrs Logan sounded tremulous as though the dance were a danger that called for all her nerve. 'You won't take Ronnie's bike, dear, will you? It's much too heavy for you.'

Vicky smiled at this concern. 'Don't worry, pettikins. I'll go carefully. It's getting back that's the trouble. The buses are hopeless.'

'Order a taxi, darling. Put it to Daddy's account.'

74

'Sweet pettikins, you know what it's like. Taxis always turn up just when you're having fun. If we have the bike, we're free.'

'Oh dear!' Mrs Logan smiled bravely at Laura. 'We must let young people enjoy themselves, mustn't we?'

Laura could see now why there was agreement between Vicky and her mother. Mrs Logan was ready to see reason while Mrs Fletcher never seemed to see it at all.

'And what about Laura?' Mrs Logan asked. 'Is she going, too?'

Laura felt excited and perturbed, seeing herself over-persuaded; Vicky running her back on the motor-bicycle to change; she changing. But into what? Not into her draggy old party dress.

Nothing happened. Vicky merely said: 'Laura can come another night.' She collected the cups on to the trolley and wheeled it back into the room. She did not return to the alcove but sauntered over to a side window and, kneeling on the window seat, gazed out as though absorbed by the house next door.

In a moment, casually, Gilda rose and went to her. The two knelt together and with their heads close, began to talk very quietly.

'Those two,' said Mrs Logan with a smile, 'they've always got secrets.' She lent towards Laura in her intimate, pleasing way and said: 'She's all we've got. We don't like her on that bike. I suppose you know about our Ronnie?'

Laura nodded her sympathy and Mrs Logan nodded, too. All Camperlea knew of Ronnie's accident. 'He's over there,' said his mother.

Laura, jerking round, saw the face of Ronnie Logan enclosed in a silver frame. He looked like Vicky and smiled like Vicky. Laura said: 'He was very good-looking.'

'Oh, ever so,' said Mrs Logan. 'All the girls were after him but he always said there was only one girl for him. He loved no one but his old mum.'

'How terrible it must have been! And sad.'

Mrs Logan raised a hand to indicate that the terror and sadness could not be described. 'We didn't want him to have that bike,' she said. 'I said: "Wait a bit Ronnie and we'll get you an M.G." But he had to have a bike. There was no stopping him. And he loved it.' Mrs Logan's sad look collapsed into gentle indulgence. 'Oh, yes, he just loved that bike.' Then she remembered how deadly that love had been and gave one of her sighs. 'Poor Vicky. It was awful for her. And now, if he'd lived, she'd have had an older brother bringing home his friends and taking her out.'

Laura nodded again. She thought of Tom and realized that his friends would not be much use to her.

Suddenly Gilda's voice rose for all to hear: 'Come on now, Vicky. Let's get your hair done before we dress.' She pulled Vicky from her perch and, both giggling, they left the room.

Laura felt she was expected to go but as she shuffled forward in her chair, preparing to say 'Thank you for having me', the front door was heard to open and shut. Mrs Logan looked round expectantly.

Laura, waiting, wondered if she were going to see the famous Mr Logan. And Mr Logan entered.

'Herbie,' his wife said happily and Mr Logan gave her a peck on the top of her head before going to a desk and starting to open letters. 'You're back nice and early.'

'Aren't we going somewhere?' said Mr Logan. 'The Collisons' cocktail party? You're ready, aren't you?'

'No, dear, but won't be a jiffy. This is Vicky's new friend, Laura.'

Laura stared, entranced by Mr Logan's pale drooping eyelids, his distinguished air, his aloof and handsome face. But Mr Logan, murmuring 'Oh?', did not turn round.

'What do you think?' Mrs Logan laughed. 'You'd never believe! Laura said to me: "I think you're wonderful, Mrs Logan. You give me hope for my old age".'

Now Mr Logan did turn. He did not smile but as he glanced at Laura, he paused and his eyes focused on her with sudden interest. He allowed her a few seconds' regard before looking away.

Laura blushed so deeply she felt faint, and croaked: 'I must go now, Mrs Logan. Thank you for having me.'

Mrs Logan, noticing nothing, said: 'Come again, dear. Good-bye and God bless.'

Reaching the hall, Laura leant against the staircase and was still standing there when Vicky and Gilda came down. Gilda was wearing silver tights and a silver jerkin; Vicky, a shift that seemed to be made of gold.

'Which way are you going?' Speaking, Vicky leant over the banister and her hair, falling forward, sheened by the iron, was as straight and almost as pale as a fall of water. Laura thought what an unimaginable fate for little Mrs Logan to marry the famous Herbert Logan and have children as beautiful as Vicky and Ronnie.

'I'm going to North Camber.'

'We could take you part of the way.'

'How could we?' Gilda impatiently asked.

'She's so small, she could sit on the tank.'

Laura broke in to say she would get the bus at the promenade.

77

'Are you sure you wouldn't like to come with us? I could lend you something. Slacks or a dress.'

'Oh, no. My mother gets worried. She's expecting me back. But could I come another time?'

Vicky smiled at the humility of this request. 'Of course you can,' she said.

Sometimes, on fine evenings, Mrs Fletcher would occupy herself in the garden. The garden was narrow and Mr Fletcher in the first ferment of marriage had planted fruit trees down each side. The trees had grown and spread. As no one knew how to prune them, they gave more foliage than fruit and their shade destroyed the central area that was known as 'the grass'. When Laura returned from the Logans, her mother was at her usual task of digging up the grass roots that luxuriated in the beds and replanting them in the lawn, where they wilted and died.

'I want to go to the St Barnabas' dances. But I must have a dress.'

'That's the next thing,' said Mrs Fletcher.

Mr Fletcher, who was tying greaseproof bands round the tree-trunks, said: 'It's to be expected. Laura's growing up.'

'But getting no sense. Where's the money to come from? I don't have a penny left at the end of the month.'

Earnestly, trying to forestall outright refusal, Laura said: 'Mummy, I do need a dress. I've hardly got anything.'

'And what have I got, I'd like to know?'

'Grief, Mummy, you don't want to go to dances!'

'Don't I? I'm not forty yet and I haven't been out since Tom was born.'

Dumbfounded by this come-back, Laura looked to her father, expecting him to defend her against injustice, but he seemed at a loss and having silenced them both, Mrs Fletcher hotly said: 'You've got enough to occupy you with your school work. Time enough for dances when you've done your O levels.'

'But after? *After* I've taken O levels?'

'We'll think about it.'

Sensing the imminence of agreement, Laura dropped down beside her mother, attempting a honey-sweet rapprochement inspired by Vicky and Mrs Logan. 'Thanks, Mummy darling, how super!' Laura put an arm round her mother's shoulder but Mrs Fletcher would not play her part. Twitching away from the embrace, she said:

'Oh, yes, you're nice enough when you're getting something. But, don't forget, the money has to come from somewhere. You can't expect us to make all the sacrifices. You'll have to help out some time. You must put your mind to your studies.'

'Oh, I do,' Laura jumped up, more vexed than her mother: 'And it's just about all I ever do.'

'You had that holiday on the Isle of Wight. *That* cost me ten pounds.'

'*Ten* pounds?'

'Yes, I sent Mrs Button the money out of my post office book.' Mrs Fletcher dug in triumph at the obdurate earth and Laura went in to do her homework.

The Upper School was subdued by the coming examinations. In the heat of midday, the girls who walked under the apple trees, walked with books in their hands. More serious students spent their luncheon hour at their desks, hands over ears. Because Gilda had to work, Vicky, too, stayed in and stared at books. They sat close together in the small front desk but towards the end of term, Mrs Logan was unwell so Vicky missed the examinations.

On the last afternoon, when all was over, Laura approached Gilda and anxiously asked: 'When's the next St Barnabas' dance?'

'There's one every week.'

'Are you going next week?'

'I really can't say.'

'I'd love to go.'

'There's nothing to stop you. They sell tickets at the door.'

Desperate, knowing the term's end would place Vicky out of reach, Laura put on her most captivating manner and said: 'Oh, Gilda, I can't go alone. Vicky said I could go with you. If I give you my address, would you pass it on to her?'

Grudgingly, Gilda said: 'I suppose so.'

Imagining her mother had the new dress in mind, Laura said at tea: 'The exams are over.'

'When do we get the results?'

'Not for ages. Can we buy the dress tomorrow?'

'What dress?'

'Oh, Mummy, you promised. *Can* we go tomorrow?'

'Tomorrow – with all the week-end shopping to be done!'

Mrs Fletcher kept to a routine that could be interrupted only after many warnings and discussions. As Laura suggested one day after another, she was told: Monday – the launderette; Tuesday – the ironing; Wednesday – the mending; Thursday – the silver to be cleaned; Friday – the milkman to be paid and shopping done; Saturday – the joint to be bought for Sunday.

'Good grief,' Laura wailed, 'can't you ditch the silver for once?'

'Any more of that sort of talk and you'll get no dress at all.'

In the end it was the silver that suffered. They went on a Thursday to a South Camperlea chain store where dresses of metallic brilliance hung on a line marked 'STRAIGHT FROM CARNABY STREET'. Laura went behind a screen and came out wearing a shift made of polyvinylchloride treated to look like gold. It had trimmings of yellow, purple and pink, and it looked to Mrs Fletcher like a cruel joke played on youth. She tried not to confirm Laura's choice by condemning the dress but could not resist saying: 'You young people have no taste.'

'You mean our taste is different from yours.' Laura stood before the glass: 'What do I look like?'

Watching Laura, her tiny body making no impact on the plastic dress, her thin legs visible to the thigh, her little hands lost in the bell-shaped sleeves, Mrs Fletcher frowned with pain and said: 'You look all right.'

The dress secured, Laura awaited a call from Vicky or Gilda, and word came even before she started to lose hope. The letter was from Gilda. Laura was summoned to hear a matter of importance. The day of invitation was Monday not Saturday, and there was no mention of the dance. Laura had no excuse to wear her golden dress.

She arrived in Flamingo Park at the given minute. As soon as she joined Vicky and Gilda on the lawn, Gilda,

82

with an important air, explained that her mother had long wished to visit her relatives in Valletta. The trip had been postponed until Gilda had taken her O levels. The examinations being over, it had been decided that she accompany her mother by air to Malta.

'How absolutely super!' breathed Laura but Gilda did not seem so sure. She shrugged and thrust out her lower lip. She appeared regretful but she was excited at the same time and conscious of being the centre of attention.

'Super, yes,' she doubtfully agreed, 'but we can't go all that way for a week or two. My mother wants to stay two months. And, you know, Mr and Mrs Logan don't like summer holidays. They go away in winter so Vicky will be here all summer.' Gilda stared directly at Laura: 'What will you be doing?'

'Me? Nothing much.' To Mrs Fletcher holidays were mere trouble and expense. Every few years, she felt bound to visit her old home, taking Laura and Tom and sometimes Mr Fletcher. When due, this dreaded event was discussed from Christmas onwards. It had not been mentioned this year so Laura could gladly say: 'I expect I'll be around. Tom and I had our holiday on the Island.'

Gilda nodded her satisfaction and Laura, amazed, realized she had been chosen as a stop-gap friend for Vicky during Gilda's absence. She wanted to shout her gratitude but instead felt it safer to deflect possible doubts by saying: 'You are lucky, Gilda. Really you are.'

'Oh, I don't know. If it weren't for my mother, nothing would get me there.'

Vicky, lying half-asleep, had let Gilda do the talking but now she mumbled: 'You're longing to go – and you know it. You can't wait to devour those Maltese boys – those dark delicious passionate Maltese ...' Vicky raised her head and was about to sit up when Gilda leapt upon her savagely.

'Liar, liar. Abominable . . . damnable . . . accursed liar!' Gripping Vicky by the shoulders and making a growling noise like a lion, Gilda nuzzled into Vicky's full, white throat while Vicky cried: 'Stop it, you goat!' and laughed in a state of near-hysteria.

Perhaps it was all a joke but it did not look like a joke to Laura.

Catching sight of Laura's startled face, Vicky struggled upright and pushing Gilda away, said: 'I don't like these rough games.' Gilda had fallen back exhausted. She held up a hand to Vicky but Vicky rose and, skirting her, ran into the house. At once Gilda sprang to her feet and shouting to Laura 'Come on', followed Vicky. As they crossed the lawn, Gilda said: 'Mrs Logan's got her bridge afternoon. Perhaps Vicky will show you her room.' She spoke as though Mrs Logan's room were territory enticing but forbidden.

'Do you mean we could dress up?' Laura asked.

Gilda laughed and sped off. Laura, running after her, reached the house as Gilda and Vicky were ascending the stairs. Gilda's arms were round Vicky and her lips against Vicky's ear. Laura could not hear what was being whispered but Vicky was smiling again, a mild and tolerant smile. They went into the big main bedroom which had the same shape and bowed alcove as the living-room. Laura, reaching the door, stared entranced at the bed flounced and padded with pale blue satin and all the other satin-flounced and padded furniture. The bed, a very large bed, was elevated upon a dais as though to emphasize the dignity of the married state. Laura imagined Mr and Mrs Logan sitting up in bed but she scarcely bothered to draw

84

in Mrs Logan. The figure she saw was Mr Logan with his drooping eyelids and aloof pale face. It seemed to her the whole room was permeated by grown-up passion and imagining the fervours of love, performed here amid so much luxury, Laura caught her breath. She knew now why Gilda had spoken as she did about Mrs Logan's room and knew why their admission to it was both a privilege and a trespass.

Vicky and Gilda went straight to the dressing-table which stood in the alcove. It was a kidney-shaped table and the most flounced and frilled object in the room.

Gilda had opened a large tortoiseshell box and was rummaging in it. 'Lots of new things,' she said. 'What's this lipstick? *Silver*. Grief, think of it? Silver lips!'

Laura, drawn out of dreams of a Mr Logan no longer aloof, no longer pale, went to search through the box with the others.

Opening and shutting little pots and boxes and cases, Gilda said: 'That's new. That's new. That's new.'

'She's always finding something new,' Vicky spoke with amused affection.

'Come on, let's have a go.' Gilda took a puff out of a bowl of powder and began to powder her face.

Trembling at such an opportunity for experiment, Laura picked among the eye-colours and said: 'Can I try some of these?'

'Here, powder first. Don't you know anything?' Gilda threw the great swansdown puff at Laura who apologized:

'It's my mother. She only lets me use lipstick. She says men like nice natural-looking girls.'

Gilda gave a howl of derision: 'That, dear child, is the last thing they like.'

When they had blotted out their faces, the three crowded

together at the glass, too absorbed to talk or laugh. Laura found a green paste flecked with gold and larded it round her eyes. She wanted gold for her lips but could not find it. Unscrewing lipstick after lipstick, she came on one that looked like mother-of-pearl. She gazed at her smudged eyes, her pearl gleaming lips, and gave a cry of delight.

'Look!' She caught Vicky's arm. Vicky looked and smiled then returned to her own employment. Watching her, Laura could see her dissatisfaction with her own perfection. Nothing could enhance the delicacy of her pink and white or the lustre of her hair; she could only change herself by subduing her look of health. She whitened her cheeks and put the silver lipstick on her mouth, put white on the bone line below her eyebrows and covered her eyelids with powdered black.

Laura was transported as Vicky changed from a creature of flesh to a nereid, the colour of a water-lily seen through the limpid folds of a stream.

As Vicky turned for the approval of the others, Laura saw that her eyes, always held to be green, were flecked with gold like mignonette. 'You are beautiful!' Laura said and Vicky bent to the glass in grave appraisal of her ethereal face, then laughed and was about to wipe it clean when Gilda commanded her: 'Put on the eye-lashes.'

Vicky took the long dark lashes from their box and put them on. Laura, seeing herself a higher authority than Gilda, said: 'Why bother? You look just as beautiful without them.'

Gilda had drawn round her eyes a black line that made her alarming. When she asked how she looked, the others stared, not knowing what to say. Laura was reminded of the Graeco-Roman ladies whose coffin-lid portraits she had seen in a library book and said: 'You look exotic.' Satisfied, Gilda returned to the box for more adornment.

Bored with make-up, Vicky opened the cupboards fitted along one wall and disclosed her mother's dresses. These were so many and so tightly packed that they showed merely as strips of velvet, silk or lace. Gilda pulled out a long evening dress and holding it before her, screamed: 'Grief, look at Grandma Hooper!' Throwing down the dress, she opened drawers and pulled out chiffon slips and night-dresses. 'I wouldn't mind some of these,' she said.

'Let's do the dance of the seven veils.' Laura gathered up handfuls of chiffon underwear and tossed them over her head, drunk with the sensuous richness of everything about her: 'Wouldn't it be beyond dreams if we lived here together, all married to one absolutely super man?'

'Thank you very much,' said Gilda in contemptuous indignation. 'I don't share anyone with anyone.'

Vicky sat on the edge of the bed to watch Laura's performance. At once Gilda threw herself on to the satin coverlet and pulling Vicky down beside her, asked: 'Would you share anyone?'

Vicky, sunken into pillows and eiderdown, vaguely said: 'I don't know. I might.'

'If you got married, would you share him?'

Vicky reflected, shrugged and laughed. The question did not rouse much interest in her.

Gilda, very close to her, urged: 'Do you want to get married? Tell me. Do you? Do you want it, really?'

Vicky shrugged again. 'I suppose so. Some time. I'd like to have children. If you don't have a family, you're pretty lonely in your old age.'

'Suppose you weren't married and someone tried to

87

make you – would you? I mean, if he were very worked up. *Would* you?'

'No.'

'You wouldn't? You mean that? You'd fight him off?'

'Yes.'

'Why?' Gilda's question seemed both a test question and a taunt.

'I've told you before why.'

'You say you would, but you couldn't. You know you couldn't.' Gilda spoke insistently, with an ardent urgency that seemed to demand a denial: 'You'd have to let him. You would, wouldn't you?'

'I wouldn't. I promise you.'

Seeing Vicky indolent and generous but adamant in preservation of an ideal privacy, Laura cried in admiration: 'Isn't she super? She wants to remain pure.'

Gilda gave a scream then collapsed with laughter, pressing her face down into Vicky's chest. Vicky smiled and said nothing. After some minutes, Gilda roused herself and began again in a low, urgent voice: 'Supposing you loved him?'

'Oh, shut up.' Vicky sounded bored with the conversation.

'Have you ever loved a man?' Gilda asked, and when Vicky shrugged again, persisted: 'Have you? Have you?'

'No.'

'Surely you love your father?' said Laura.

Vicky impassively replied: 'Of course. Don't you love yours?'

'Yes, but mine's quite old. I mean, no one would . . . no one . . .'

'Ha!' Gilda pounced on Laura's confusion: 'She's fallen for Herbie. Would you believe it?'

Laura blushed but the others were not interested in her self-betrayal. Though pressed so closely against Vicky, Gilda wriggled as though she would, if she could, press closer. She whispered: 'Supposing someone, someone madly exciting, touched you *there*!'

'Do shut up.'

Taking this for encouragement, aglow with excitement, Gilda lifted herself over Vicky and whispered so Laura could not hear. Vicky lay unmoved, her gaze on the ceiling, but she was smiling all the time. Suddenly the door of the room opened and Mrs Logan came in.

Laura stood up nervously, expecting trouble, but at the sight of the two girls sprawled on the pale blue counterpane, Mrs Logan merely laughed: 'Did you ever see the like! What've you got on your faces? You've been at my box, I bet. And what's all this on the floor? There's a way to treat my best nighties. You're naughty girls. Come on. Get up off of there if you want your tea.'

When neither girl attempted to move, Mrs Logan gave Gilda a slap on the backside and Gilda whooped and shrieked.

'Now, get up. The trolley's in.' Mrs Logan spoke more seriously and Vicky and Gilda slowly disentangled their limbs and removed themselves from the bed.

Here, Laura thought, life was lived as it should be lived. There were no anxieties, no bad temper, no worrying about wear and tear and the need to save money. The Logans seemed to her the denizens of paradise. Could she, she wondered, stay long enough to see Mr Logan again? When, after tea, Vicky took her friends up to her bedroom to play records, Laura went in fear of missing his return home. But he was not returning that evening. He was,

Vicky happened to mention, in London. Apparently he often went to London.

Laura, in an uneven voice, asked: 'What does he do there?'

'Who knows?' Vicky laughed at the question. 'No one knows what *he*'s up to.'

Laura was silent, disturbed by the thought of Mr Logan 'up to' something in London; then it occurred to her that when she went to London herself, she might see him there. She had a vision of meeting Mr Logan in some splendid Soho street and Mr Logan saying: 'Well, this is a surprise! How about coming to the Ritz with me?'

Gilda was saying: 'I'll be here for the Summer Dance, anyway. Not that that means much.'

'Can I come?' Laura begged. 'I've got a new dress.'

Gilda raised her brows in tantalizing uncertainty. 'I don't think so. It's a special dance. You might say it's an X certificate dance.'

'What does that mean?'

'The vicar's invited some big rough men. They'd be too wild for a little girl like you.'

Laura looked anxiously at Vicky who said that as a gesture against Camperlea snobbery, the vicar had written to the Salthouse factory inviting some of the men to the dance. 'I don't expect anything will come of it. They'll be too shy.'

'The vicar's grotty,' said Gilda in disgust. 'He makes us have a waltz before the interval and another waltz at the end. The curate said: "What young people want is more Detroit," but the vicar will have this waltz stuff. He's crumbling, if you ask me.'

Vicky said: 'But the curate's super.'

'Yes, super,' Gilda agreed. 'He looks smashing in church gear.'

'*Can't* I come?' Laura pleaded.

Vicky laughed: 'Don't be a goose. Of course you can.'

To be, even briefly and only by proxy, the friend of Victoria Logan gave Laura the sense that life had begun. For this beginning she could, she supposed, thank Mrs Toplady and the dolls in the Play Room.

Before this, it seemed to her, the possibilities of life had been packed up tight in her, a core of discontent. Now, like a Japanese paper flower that opens in water, the core was opening and expanding and taking on colour. Anything might come of it. *Anything*.

At home she tried on her golden dress and critically viewed her image in the bathroom mirror. Already the worse for trying on, the dress lay as flat as a saucepan lid on her little bosom. Next day, wandering round Woolworth's with the feverish expectation of an Idea, she saw some foam rubber mats of different sizes and the Idea came. The mats were table mats, but Laura saw another use for them. Whatever the source of inspiration – Mrs Toplady was still with her although out of sight like a piece of old underwear stuffed under a cushion – she bought six mats, two of each size, on which to experiment. Snipping a V in each, she turned them into cones. Fitting three cones together, she produced a satisfactory mammalian image which she duplicated with the other three. These had taken more than enough of her pocket money but, in order to wear them, she would have to buy a brassière. The expense was painful but the final effect delighted her. Then she wondered how was she to explain this overnight development? She would have to be bold. If she were not, the best part of ten shillings would have been thrown away.

When Laura came down dressed and ready for the dance, Mrs Fletcher stared in amazement then asked: 'What ever has the girl been up to?'

Mr Fletcher, with Sugarpuss on his knee, could see nothing amiss. 'That's a nice dress,' he said, then dozed off again.

Laura looked at her mother abashed, so abashed that Mrs Fletcher let the matter drop. 'Who's going with you?' she asked.

'Vicky Logan and Gilda Hooper.'

The grandeur of these names was lost on Mrs Fletcher. 'Vicky Logan,' she repeated with distaste. 'You know, that Ronnie Logan used to go like a maniac on that motor-bicycle. I'm not surprised at what happened.'

Laura said proudly: 'Vicky rides it now.'

Mrs Fletcher was aghast: 'You mean, she rides the bicycle her brother was killed on?'

'Why not? The bicycle wasn't hurt. She found it hidden in the garden shed and she got a friend to teach her to ride it. She takes Gilda on the back.'

'I've never heard a more disgraceful thing! A girl going about on the bike that killed her brother!'

'Oh, Mummy, you're impossible. If someone gets killed in a car, you don't throw the car away. Do you?'

'Don't let me ever hear of you going on it.'

Laura sighed: 'It's not safe to tell you anything.'

In her eagerness to be at the dance, Laura reached the Logans' house half an hour early. No one answered her knock. She tried the door handle and when the door opened, went in and paused at the foot of the staircase, conscious of being alone amid splendour. Vicky would be

92

upstairs dressing. Regal with her gold dress over her foam bosom, Laura went up, her dancing-class sandals noiseless on the carpet. She decided that at the top she would come face to face with Mr Logan. They would stop and stare at each other, she radiant, he stunned.

Alas, there was no Mr Logan at the top. All the doors were shut. Should she call 'Vicky' or tap on Vicky's door? As she stood uncertain which action would be correct, a thin cry came from behind the door, rising and eddying up in ecstatic agony, forming the words, 'Darling ... darling ... darling', then sinking down to nothingness.

Laura held her breath, expecting something more, but there was only silence. She had never before heard so abandoned a cry. As the silence was protracted, it seemed to her she had heard something supernatural. She whispered 'Beyond dreams', and felt both frightened and inspired. Then the strangeness of the experience stirred her and she wanted to get away. Turning to run, she struck her hand against a consol table and a voice spoke in the room: 'Grief, there's someone outside.'

Laura fled down to the living-room then wished she had escaped into the garden. Gilda was out at once. She shouted over the banister: 'Who's there?'

Laura edged into the hall and whispered: 'Me.'

'Oh, it's you, is it?'

With Gilda's calculating and accusing stare upon her, Laura could only apologize: 'I was early. I came upstairs. Is Vicky ill?'

Pacified by Laura's manner, Gilda became confidential: 'As a matter of fact, she is. The sun's been too much for her. She's lying down for a bit.

'Is she delirious?'

'Um. Well! Slightly.'

'So she can't come to the dance?'

'Oh, yes, she'll soon be all right. You wait there. I'm going to iron her hair. We won't be long.'

Wandering among the chairs and ornamental tables, Laura met Ronnie's pleasant smile. Supposing, supposing, supposing Ronnie Logan were still alive! Mr Logan had the fascination of his importance, but Ronnie would be free. Laura stood for a long time gazing back at Ronnie whose photograph had the faded, enervated bloom that overlies photographs of the dead. He seemed to be watching her from another world, perhaps a more desirable world. Bemused, Laura envisaged him as friend, as lover, as husband, becoming so immersed in her fantasy that she was jolted by the arrival of Mr Logan. He was not the person she had expected.

'Where's everyone?' he asked.

The reality of Herbert Logan at once extinguished poor ghostly Ronnie. Laura, gulping down her excitement, told him that Vicky and Gilda were upstairs dressing.

'We're going to a dance,' she said.

'You're all dressed up for a dance, are you?' Mr Logan looked Laura over with a serious expression that rested on her bosom. Remembering there was more of her, he hurriedly looked down at her long, exposed legs, and said: 'Very smart.' Unfortunately his glance was attracted back to the bosom that, constructed with the resource of deprivation, was now worth more attention than Laura herself.

She turned away and walked into the alcove. He asked: 'Do you know where my wife is?'

'I don't think she's in. I haven't seen anyone but Gilda.'

Mr Logan went to his desk and more at ease now, asked: 'Have you seen my plan for the York Street extension of the public baths? Come over here.' His manner was light, almost joking, but Laura went reluctantly, feeling his presence was strain enough; if she went nearer to him, she might stifle with her own perturbation.

He was putting paper-weights on the top corners of the plan and holding the lower edge with a long elegant hand. His other hand indicated the old swimming-bath then, moving a delicate pointed finger, he outlined the extension that would be used for public meetings. Apparently absorbed in his explanation, he interposed with no change of tone: 'You'll be breaking all hearts tonight.'

Laura exploded in giggles, then tried to regain her dignity: 'How could I with Vicky there? I'm not beautiful. Besides, I'm too thin.'

'But this,' Mr Logan's hand wavered above Laura's foam-filled dress-top, '*This* is delicious.'

Laura took a step back. She was terrified that Mr Logan would do something violent. He might try and pull her dress down. Imagining his sense of outrage when he discovered the deception, she almost confessed to it there and then, but before she could speak, he returned to the plan and calmly asked: 'Do you ever go to the swimming-bath?'

'No, I don't like that stuff in the water.'

'Chlorine?' he laughed and let the plan go. As it curled itself up, he patted his pockets. Laura thought he was looking for cigarettes and was taken off guard when he scized her and kissed her on the mouth with professional ardour.

She could appreciate the incident only when it was over; then, realizing that Mr Logan, of all people, had kissed her, she wanted him to repeat the embrace. *Slowly*. She looked up at him, lifting her hands, but he made a movement of warning.

Vicky and Gilda were coming down the stairs.

He sauntered over to the alcove and with languid grace, dropped into the chair where Mrs Logan usually sat. Lying there with his air of detached composure, he glanced round to see Vicky, saying: 'So you're off to a dance, I hear.' While he made some joking remarks about the sufferings of young men and the sadly flirtatious nature of pretty girls, Laura, unnoticed, recovered as best she could. She was still trembling when, in the garden, she watched Ronnie's famous motor-bicycle being wheeled out of the garden shed. At the sight of the big B.S.A., her admiration surpassed itself. What other pampered girl would dare to ride this machine? Vicky was not only kind and beautiful, she was an independent and intrepid spirit. She was a heroine.

Gilda, less admiring, crossly asked: 'How can you pack us all on?'

'Laura will be all right on the tank. She's a sparrow-weight. The only thing is, she'll have to keep her head down.'

Mrs Fletcher had placed her ban on the motor-bicycle but Laura had made no promises. Crouched astride the tank, gripping the centre of the handle-bars, her precarious and uncomfortable seat was all part of this amazing evening. Riding along the front, they were watched by every male in sight. The trip to St Barnabas' Church Hall was hilarious. Gilda, on the pillion, screamed each time they swung round a corner and shouted to every personable boy they passed. Laura, still under the influence of Mr Logan's gallantry, was impressed by Gilda's uninhibited display. She was sure now that Gilda spoke the truth when she said the boys were all mad for her.

When they reached the church, Gilda screamed: 'We've

made it.' Alerted, the young men loitering under the churchyard trees, came to the wall to watch the girls' arrival. Laura, never before seen in such conspicuous company, was pink with pride as she followed Vicky and Gilda across the grass. The hall was no bigger than an army hut. Bunting hung from the rafters and behind the stage used by the pop group there was a giant Union Jack with a notice to say it had been presented by Lieutenant-Commander Loopey, R.N. (ret.), on Empire Day 1930.

'Grief,' breathed Laura. 'Isn't it super!'

The four men of the group that called itself 'The Water Beetles' wore long-haired blond wigs and old frock-coats in recognition of a neoteric mood that, so far, had made little progress in Camperlea. The dance had started. They were already making all the noise they could.

Surveying everything in buoyant expectation, Laura was surprised when the gaiety did not go on. Vicky was claimed at once by Dick Garside, the Head Boy at Camperlea College, and when she went on to the floor, Gilda took herself off to talk to some college boys. Laura, left alone, did not know what to do with her own high spirits. Sitting against the wall, smiling as though nothing mattered, she watched Vicky and Dick leave the floor and go into a corner where they appeared to be arguing in a despondent way. When she grew tired of sitting, Laura went to read a notice headed SOMETHING FOR EVERYONE in which the vicar said he did not object to modern dancing but the young must think of the not-so-young and join in the ballroom dancing as well. She was reminded of the invitation sent to the Salthouse factory men and looked about her but she saw only the South Camperlea boys who dressed like their fathers and were content, it seemed, to follow the vicar's precept.

An hour or more passed before two Salthouse guests appeared. Laura, very bored, was stimulated by the sight of them. Each Camperlea man seemed bound to one particular girl friend but as the Salthouse men knew no one here, surely one of them would dance with Laura! But no. They simply stood in the doorway watching the hall with derisive unbelief, then one laughed outright, the other pulled him away and in a moment they were gone. Laura returned her attention to Vicky and Dick who danced only with each other when not standing together in argument. Clearly it was a disintegrating relationship and Laura thought how wonderful it would be if Vicky would come over and tell her all about it.

When the music changed for the pre-interval waltz, Vicky and Dick drifted round, gazing at each other as though fascinated by the whole sad, unsatisfactory situation.

Laura, also fascinated, had given up hope of dancing and so was startled to find a new arrival standing in front of her, indicating with a jerk of the head that he was willing to partner her in the waltz. He was a Salthouse man. The other two had been dressed in Salthouse finery but this one was exceptional only in wearing a turtle-neck shirt. Laura leapt up. He scooped her to him and holding her so tightly she could not move her body, began to rock and sway to a rhythm of his own. Laura tried to fit her steps to his but found it difficult to shut out the music of the waltz.

Their feet clashed and to divert him, she asked: 'Do you come from London?'

He made a noise in his throat that told her nothing.

'You do come from the factory, don't you?'

'Ye-ah.'

98

His head was a long way above her. Leaning back in order to study him, she saw that his pallid features and dark hair had distinction of a sort. He was rough and over-muscled; his eyes, dark and avid, were fixed on anything but Laura. Yet he was a prize.

She said: 'We've got a cat called Sugarpuss.'

The information was slow to reach him. When it did, he looked down on her, frowning, obviously thinking she was deranged. She laughed at having caught his attention.

'Don't you like cats?' she asked.

'Cats? How do I know?'

His voice was slow and nasal. He did not want to discuss cats or anything else.

Laura persisted: 'Haven't you got a cat at home?'

'Nope. No cats where I come from.'

'Where *do* you come from?'

He looked down again and this time his black stare was angry and suspicious: 'What's that to do with you?'

The rebuff stopped her questions. She let herself be pulled round in discomfort while he stared over her head. As she regained audacity, she thought to lighten the atmosphere with a little feminine flirtatiousness. At the next collision of feet, she gave a loud yelp.

'Something bite you?' he sourly asked.

'You trod on me. I must say, you're a vile waltzer.'

He did not reply. The music was banging to a close. At the last note, he dropped her without a word and walked out of the hall. Abandoned, Laura looked round with a startled laugh then, blessedly, was caught up in the movement towards a side room where voluntary helpers sold buns and coffee.

Vicky and Dick did not appear in the refreshment-room.

Gilda, in spite of her power over the male sex, came in alone. Ironically, looking Laura over, she said: 'So you did get a dance, after all!'

'I don't know anyone.'

'You don't have to. Go and talk to them the way I do. They can't eat you.'

Laura was not sure. She felt as though her waltz partner had eaten her or, at any rate, bitten her head off. Gilda remained standing with her but kept a watch over the shifting crowd in hope of better company. Laura did not know for whom she was looking until she said: 'Where's your fellow? He looked like something. You might introduce me.'

'I don't know where he is. He went out.'

'Off to the pub, I shouldn't wonder.'

Had she not had company in the interval, Laura would probably have gone home in despair. As it was, following Gilda back to the hall, she found herself at the centre of drama. Vicky, seeing her friends, came at once to join them. Dick Garside, a very fair boy of appearance so flawless he seemed to Laura beyond human desiring, remained on the other side of the room. He was soon surrounded by youths who gazed askance at Vicky, Gilda and Laura. Though his friends were indignant on his behalf, Dick was too hurt or too high-minded to display any feeling at all.

Gilda seemed to know what it was all about. Laura could only wonder, for Vicky explained nothing. Sitting with Gilda on her right and Laura on her left, she looked remote and pensive, somehow implying that Dick Garside and his court were no concern of hers. It was getting late. Dance or no dance, Laura had to be home by half past ten. If later she would suffer the penalty of her mother's anxiety.

She whispered that she had better go but Vicky said: 'Wait, I'll run you part of the way.'

They went on sitting, Vicky silent but observed by all. Though she had left Dick, she apparently wished to remain in his view. If a male approached, Gilda would say they were not dancing. Laura, who had danced so little, felt now in the aura of majesty. It would have been splendid had she not been so worried about getting home. Then, suddenly, Vicky rose and said: 'We'll go.' With her female attendants behind her, she left the hall, making her queenly progress amid the glances of the men.

Out in the churchyard, in the mild, sweet-smelling summer darkness, Laura hoped she would at last hear what had occurred; but Gilda would permit no open discussion. With her usual possessive secrecy, she put her arm round Vicky's neck and began to whisper; Vicky, from habit, whispered her replies.

They walked so slowly that Laura felt bound to go ahead along the churchyard path. The street lights, breaking and raying among the churchyard trees, gave intermittent light that showed the bulky shape of a yew tree. When she reached it, a man stepped from the shadow and blocked her way, saying:

'I want a word with you.'

Laura looked behind for the protection of her companions but they, following a policy of non-intervention in affairs of the heart, slipped round the yew and disappeared down the path. Laura tried to follow them but her interceptor moved in front of her, saying, 'No you don't.' His tone was ominous. The street light touched his face. She saw he was the Salthouse man with whom she had danced.

He said: 'You called me a vile walsop. I want to know what you mean by it.'

'I called you *what*?'

'You heard me. It was a dead liberty, saying a thing like that.'

'But what did I say?'

'Don't give me that. You know what you said.'

She backed away, but the accusation seemed to her so baseless, she was more bewildered than alarmed. As she stepped back, he advanced on her and she saw that his face had become misshapen with anger at her inability to explain. 'You tell me what you meant or else.'

She pleaded, becoming frightened: 'But I don't know. I didn't call you anything.'

'"Vile walsop" was what you said.'

'How do you spell it?'

'I don't spell it.'

She shook her head helplessly, remembering nothing that could account for the charge. She tried to laugh, thinking her feminine powers might get her out of this predicament, and saying: 'Really, you're being silly,' she dodged round the tree but was caught at once. His fingers, like a gyve on her arm, destroyed her faith in her feminine powers. Whimpering 'Please let me go', she pulled away, prepared to scream. As she opened her mouth, she saw that Vicky had come back along the path and was standing a few yards away. Her scream became 'Vicky, Vicky, Vicky' and her assailant jerked round to see who was behind him. At the sight of Vicky, lit by the street lamp as by a spotlight, he released Laura who sped away, crying in panic, 'Run, Vicky, run. He's mad', but Vicky did not move.

'What is happening?' she asked, smiling in reproof, as

though she had witnessed nothing worse than a breach of good manners.

'He says I called him something. I didn't. I didn't.'

'I'm sure you didn't.' Vicky put out her hand and let Laura hold it, but she remained where she was, her face lifted in amusement, her hair blown back by the wind, her dress, blown against her body, revealing the delicate line of her breast curving in to her very small waist. The young man stared, his face blank as the face of an idiot.

'I must go,' Laura quavered. 'I have to be home by half past ten.'

Still smiling, Vicky made a move of good-humoured impatience: 'Come along then. Gilda and I got tired of waiting. I thought I'd better see what was keeping you.' She turned, taking Laura with her, and as they went to the gate, they heard the man following behind. 'He's crazy,' Laura whispered. 'He hurt my arm. I'm sure he's bruised it.'

Gilda was sulking beside the motor-bicycle.

'All aboard, then,' Vicky said and Laura hoped they would speed off at once. The others surely were as eager as she was to escape the fiend in the rear; but, instead, Vicky glanced over her shoulder smiling, and when she saw him, smiled the more.

He was watching Vicky with his avid eyes. 'That your machine?' he asked.

Vicky nodded.

'Old-time model, eh?'

'It's six years old. It hasn't been ridden much.'

'Not a bike for a chick like you.'

'I can manage it.'

He half smiled, but grudgingly as though a complete smile would be too much to give. 'You come here often?'

'Most weeks.'

'You never been to the factory dance? That's something. That's where it is. None of this ballroom lark. No la-di-dah stuff. We don't have birds sitting out like she was' – he gave a contemptuous nod at Laura. 'With us, we dance how we like. Dance by yourself, if you like. We shift about, too. Anyone alone, we shift over, give them a break. Our pop is pop. We keep jumping. It's wild.'

'Oh!'

'A bird like you's wasted in this dump.'

Vicky, smiling, stood and listened as though entranced. Laura, too, was listening but Gilda nudged her and reminded her of time's passing: 'We'd better start walking. Looks as though we won't get a lift tonight.'

'You will. I'm coming.' Vicky put her leg over the saddle but even when they were all in place, she did not move.

'Three girls on a bike.' The man spoke with gleeful disbelief: '*This* I must see.'

'What's your name?' Vicky asked.

'Piper. Clarrie Piper.'

'Clarrie? How did you get a name like Clarrie?'

'That's what they called me.'

Vicky kicked the starter and as they moved off, he shouted: 'Come to our scene next Saturday. I'll be watching for you.'

'I'll think about it.'

Having delayed Laura, Vicky, from charity, drove her back to the top of Rowantree Avenue and leaving her there, said: 'Give me a ring next week.'

Before receiving this command, Laura had not given much thought to the telephone. Now, seeing it as a lifeline, she said next day: 'Why haven't we got a telephone?'

'A telephone! That,' said Mrs Fletcher with satisfaction, 'is one thing we can do without.'

Monday was the day Gilda flew to Malta. Laura waited till Tuesday before going to the call-box in Gladstone Road. The small red houses of the side roads were glowing with early evening. Children out for their after-tea play hour were shouting and chasing each other from pavement to pavement. As one small girl cranked past on a model motor-car, Laura wondered if anyone had ever made a model motor-bike. Smiling above the trivialities of childhood, breathing in the scent of jasmine and syringa that came in wafts from alleyways and corner gardens, Laura imagined a future full of romantic emotions, a future that held someone who looked exactly like Mr Logan.

The call-box, empty for once, stood outside a corner shop that was toyshop, stationers and post office all in one. It had once been a shop important to Laura on pocket-money days. She must have spent a fortune there on rolls of coloured paper from which she and Valerie Whittam had made dresses for plays written by Laura. The plays were acted in the Fletchers' back garden for the delectation of no one but Mr Fletcher who, sitting in a deck-chair, solitary as Ludwig II in his private theatre, usually fell asleep after the first ten minutes.

Those days were over. Laura intended one day to write grown-up plays that would rock much vaster audiences but at the moment her right hand was trembling as she put the money in the box and dialled Vicky's number. She thought Vicky might say 'Get on the bus and come down now' but Vicky, when she answered, had no time to talk. In the background there were lively voices and bursts of laughter. Laura said: 'Are you having a party?'

'Oh, just some of Daddy's friends in for drinks. Come and have tea one day. Could you come Friday?'

'Yes, of course.'

'Great. Come early. Must fly. Mummy wants me to hand round the eats. Bye.'

'Bye, Vicky. Bye.' Friday seemed a long way off.

Laura, at home all day, was required to do the shopping and go with the washing to the launderette. Sometimes Mr Fletcher went with her but he found that these days Laura's company had lost its zest. Drawn by all her desires towards Flamingo Park, she could scarcely keep from jumping aboard when she saw a southbound bus. She could imagine her father watching after it, bewildered but without vexation, and she felt ashamed of the impulse to leave him. If only they lived in South Camperlea, they might meet Vicky or Mr Logan in the street. Here, at the wrong end of the town, there was no one to fill the High Road's crowded emptiness. Whenever she could, she went to the reading room that, created by Mr Logan, seemed to breathe his essence. There, when she had changed her library books, she looked through *Vogue* and *Harper's* and studied pictures of the people who lived in London. The whole population of London, apparently, was young and beautiful but no one, it seemed to her, was as beautiful as Vicky.

While she was listing the boutiques in Chelsea, intending, as a first essay, to find work in one of them, she suddenly came to a stop and wondered if she could possibly leave Camperlea if Vicky would not leave with her. If she were really Vicky's friend, would Vicky let her go? And if Vicky held her, would she want to go? Plagued by uncertainty, she gazed out at the municipal compost heap and knew there was only one solution. Vicky's uninterest must be overcome. Vicky must be persuaded to London.

Friday afternoon was damp and dull. Mrs Logan had visitors in the living-room and the girls went to Vicky's bedroom where the furniture was white and the wallpaper, curtains and coverlet all had the same pattern of corn-flowers.

With Gilda gone, Laura had imagined that she and Vicky would be like runaways from a tyrant, full of talk and congratulatory jollity. They were nothing of the sort. Vicky threw herself on the bed in abstracted mood, leaving Laura to make what conversation she could.

Mrs Logan's women friends could be heard, voices raised in their efforts to reveal themselves, but Vicky had no wish to reveal herself and she demanded no revelations from Laura. Laura had longed to have Vicky to herself and now they were alone, she found Vicky's company disturbing but not inspiriting. Vicky's languor infected her. Unable to think of anything to say, she looked through the gramophone records and asked: 'Shall I put one on?' Vicky murmured: 'If you like,' obviously too lazy even to listen. Gilda had known how to awaken Vicky. Without Gilda, Vicky would make no effort, yet she had been animated enough when talking to Clarrie Piper. Laura did not want to remember Clarrie but he was something she could talk about.

She said: 'That man at the dance – Clarrie Piper! Do you think he was crazy?'

Vicky's lips parted. She seemed about to speak but instead she swallowed in her throat and a flush rose in her cheeks and, slowly spreading, displaced the milky pallor of her throat.

Astonished, Laura said: 'Grief! You weren't struck, were you?'

'Didn't you think him attractive?'

'No, I didn't. I've still got a mark where he clutched my arm.'

'Were you scared?'

'Well, who wouldn't be? But I knew you weren't far away.'

'Gilda wanted to go. Supposing we'd given you up! Supposing you'd been alone with him!'

'I'd have been pretty scared, yes.'

'What did he say you called him?'

'A vile walsop. I've never heard of such a thing.'

'Neither have I. I suppose it's some new word they use at the factory. It could be hip.'

'He didn't look hip to me. I thought him a drag.'

'But supposing you'd been alone with him? Wouldn't you've been terrified?'

'Perhaps. But I was thinking of putting my teeth into his hand. That would have made him yell.'

Vicky stared at the ceiling, frowning a little at this demotion of Clarrie's image, then, after a moment, said: 'But he was dishy. You have to admit that.'

'Not my dish. Lots of men are better-looking. Dick Garside is. So's your father.' Laura would have been happy now to discuss Mr Logan in relation to lesser men, but Vicky would not leave the subject of Clarrie Piper.

'It wasn't just his looks. There was something about him – something ...' In her effort to define Clarrie Piper's quality, Vicky drew in her breath, then said: 'Something savage. He was extraordinary. Beyond dreams.'

'Not for me.'

Smiling at her memory of Clarrie Piper, Vicky sat up, suddenly animated, and said: 'You really hated him, didn't you?'

Laura realized that the more violent the emotion roused by Clarrie, the more splendid he would seem to Vicky. Struck with jealousy of him, she refused to join this game of enhancing him and shrugged her indifference: 'Not really. I thought he was stupid.'

Vicky laughed: 'I wouldn't call him stupid. Let's take another look at him. Let's go there tomorrow night.'

'To the factory dance? Both of us?'

'Natch.'

'But he didn't ask me.'

'Of course he did. He invited us all. I wouldn't go there alone.'

When Laura said nothing, Vicky asked: 'Didn't you enjoy the church dance?'

'There wasn't much to enjoy. No one danced with me except Clarrie Piper and you saw what came of that.'

'Was Clarrie the only one you danced with? I didn't know. Dick Garside was being a drag. He was trying to pin me down ... trying to make me say I loved him and all that mush. I was so bored, I just said we'd break it off. But I didn't know you'd had a dismal night, really I didn't.'

'Oh, well! I'm sorry about Dick Garside. He looks so super.'

'He looks all right, but he's slug. And so are those church dances. Clarrie Piper was right. They're slug as hell.'

'It's Camperlea,' said Laura, eager in concurrence. 'Everything's slug in Camperlea. Nothing happens here. It's years behind the times. It's ... it's provincial.'

'Provincial? Of course it's provincial.'

'Yes, but it doesn't have to be as provincial as this. You know, Vicky, there's only one place really! That's London. In Soho there are places that stay open all night. You don't have to go to bed at all. This town's like a morgue by ten o'clock. When I leave school, I'm going straight to London. Come with me, Vicky. *Do* come. Let's go to London together.'

Vicky lay smiling up at the ceiling but she answered seriously: 'I couldn't. My mother wants me here. But you don't mean it, do you? What about your mother? Surely you don't want to leave her?'

Laura was about to say 'It's because of her I want to go', but she paused, knowing the statement to be unjust. She loved her mother, loved and pitied her. She would say nothing against her. 'I'd come back at week-ends, of course; but one has to live one's own life. And I hate Camperlea. It's a smothering place. You can't do anything here.'

'Oh, I don't know. It's not bad.'

Laura could see that viewed from Flamingo Park, Camperlea was different from the Camperlea she saw. A bed-sitter in London was not so enticing when one had been used to the splendours of the Logan household, yet she said persuasively: '*Do* come.'

'We'll think about it. You won't be going for years, anyway.' Vicky was clearly bored by Laura's talk of London and turning to smile at her, said: 'Meanwhile, there's lots of fun here. We'll go and see what happens at Salthouse. We needn't stay if we don't like it. We'll just put our heads in.'

Laura nodded without enthusiasm: 'All right.'

'After all,' Vicky was now the persuader, 'most of the

factory men were brought here from London. My father says Salthouse is a London suburb now. I bet Clarrie Piper comes from London. You can ask him about it.'

'I asked him but he wouldn't tell me anything. In fact, he was horrible.'

'Didn't you talk about anything?'

'I talked about cats.'

'Cats! You didn't. You're cuckoo.' Vicky laughed at her absurdity and as she laughed, she rolled on to her back in an attitude that troubled Laura with a memory of something that had been almost but not quite relegated to her unconscious. Gazing at Vicky's perfect body, her long arms and long legs sprawled on the cornflower-patterned counterpane, Laura suddenly remembered the Play Room. Those abominable dolls! Touched with repulsion, she said: 'About tomorrow. I don't think I can go. My mother's always fussing. I don't know what she'd say if I told her I was going to a factory dance.'

'Grief! You don't mean to say you'd *tell* her?'

'Wouldn't you tell your mother?'

'Of course not. You are a baby. If Dad and I let Mummy know half the things we do, she'd die.'

At this hint of Mr Logan's habitual deception, Laura could not speak but her face spoke for her and Vicky said: 'I didn't realize you were so slug.'

'I'm *not* slug. It's just that I didn't think of not telling. But supposing she asks?'

'She won't. They know we go to the St Barnabas' Dance and they'll take it for granted that's where we're going on Saturday. You want to come with me, don't you? All right. I'll pick you up at your house, if you like.'

'Grief, no. My mother's funny about motor-bicycles.'

'At the end of the road, then. Seven sharp.'

Laura nodded but now their moods had been exchanged. She was apathetic while Vicky, a-shimmer with anticipation, was eager for Laura to share her eagerness. 'You'll see, we'll have a fabulous time. It'll be mad. I'll make Clarrie introduce you to everyone. If you don't dance, I won't dance either.'

Ravished by these promises, Laura forgot the Play Room and remembered she was Vicky's friend. Vicky had lent her a handkerchief and she, in return, would go wherever Vicky wanted her to go.

Laura had not been to Salthouse for three years. She was reluctant to return there but could not remember why. Salthouse had changed and seemed frightening, perhaps, merely because unfamiliar. Years ago, when Mr Fletcher had gone with the children for Sunday walks, they used to take the bus to the level crossing and then find themselves in a country district, adventurous with tumble-down neglect. There had been clay pits and a brickworks and the great hangar where the sea-planes were serviced. But the whole of Salthouse was now in the hands of the developers. The downland slopes had been eaten up by the housing estate. The road had ceased to be a country road and had become a highway for the factory lorries that went up to join the Brighton road above. The last time she was there the factory foundations had just been laid. It was an important factory that made plastic and plastic goods. A whole population had been brought to Salthouse during the last three years. What had once been a playground for North Camperlea was now a township of council houses and plain utilitarian buildings.

The *Camperlea Herald* had spoken of the 'new, raw, unconventional Salthouse community'. Well and good. The trouble was not that the Salthouse people were new, raw and unconventional but that they had so much money to spend. The women, large, loud bursting girls in slacks and high-heeled shoes, would come to the High Street on Saturday afternoons and go back laden with meat, poultry, fruit, tinned vegetables, cakes and sweetmeats. Their homeward cavalcade was a vision of abundance that astounded the Camperlea pensioners. Still carefully making do themselves, they scarcely knew that prosperity had overtaken other places.

Mrs Fletcher, who had an ingrained habit of putting away for a 'rainy day', said: 'Those women never save a penny.'

Laura, ready to take any view so long as it was opposed to the Camperlea view, defended the Salthouse spend-thrifts ('If they have the money, why shouldn't they enjoy it') while distrusting them. Salthouse, though another world, was not the world she wanted.

Early on Saturday evening, when the shops were shutting and the pavements were dusty and paper-strewn, Vicky and Laura rode out of the town, passing the gas-works and crossing the channel that divided Camperlea from Salthouse. Topping the bridge, that was railway- and foot-bridge, Laura, on the pillion, looked over the broad, shallow mud basin of Salthouse Creek and saw in the distance the black shape of the Salthouse hangar.

The tide was out. The basin was nothing now but inter-folding curves of mud, all bright with evening, and a

113

stream that hurried after the retreating sea. At high tide, the sea would flow back and the whole large basin would turn into a lake. Mr Fletcher had told Tom and Laura that before the war the channel had been dammed and the creek used as an anchorage for sea-planes. When the naval experimental unit left Camperlea, the winter seas broke the dam and now the sea flowed in and the stream flowed out just as they had done since time began.

On the other side of the bridge was the level crossing and once over this, they were in Salthouse with the new factory and the cinema and the public house and a few small shops. The childhood world of Laura, Tom and Mr Fletcher was all built over and no one from Camperlea came here now. Half-way down the road, the girls heard the thud-thud of the factory pop group. The whole street seemed a-tremble with it as with the excitement of riot and Laura's spirits rose. They did not need to ask where the dance was. Uproar came from a brick-built hall opposite the factory, no bigger than the church hall but extruding a sense of crowded vitality. Some of the men were standing outside and when Vicky stopped the machine at the kerb, they came down the steps and drifted towards her as though pulled by some power that came from her. They looked inquiring, red-faced, yearning as dogs, all their eyes upon her. When near enough, the first one said with unbelieving awe: 'You for the dance, miss?' Vicky smiled and nodded. While the first man spoke, the others pressed forward, all bent towards Vicky as though to say: 'What do you want? What can we do?' They were hot with admiration.

Laura, observant but not observed, could see what it was like to be Vicky. It seemed to her the whole of Vicky's life would be one long reward for being beautiful. Where-ever Vicky went, she would receive gratitude for being Vicky – and that was as it should be.

Vicky asked: 'Is there a car park?' Several of them pointed to the bare, wired-in ground beside the hall but the first man already had his hands on the machine. He held to it, saying: 'Here, let's run it in for you.'

Vicky let the bicycle go without another glance. She had received so much approval in her life, she could scarcely know the world held anything else. As she walked to the door with Laura a step behind her, the men followed at a respectful distance but jostled together in recognition of the opportunity she might present.

Inside the entrance hall, where someone was selling tickets, the eldest man, who must have been twenty, took the matter over as by right. 'Looking for anyone in particular, miss?' he asked.

'We were invited by Mr Clarrie Piper.'

'Old Clarrie?'

Laura heard a disparaging mutter among the group behind but still they were ready to serve. The elderly youth said: 'He's here somewhere.' The music had stopped for a moment and the men shouted into the hall: 'Hi, Clarrie.' 'Clarrie, you're wanted.' 'Over here, you lucky basket.'

Clarrie Piper, with aloof blank face, came to the door and pushed between the men who eyed and encouraged him with a half-jeering envy.

Laura could see he did not know what to expect. She felt their dislike of him. He was holding himself taut, knowing it might all be a joke, a piece of cruelty, but when he saw Vicky his front collapsed. For an instant he looked anguished, then he gave a brief smile, vain and gratified. 'Looking for me?'

115

'Weren't you expecting us?' Vicky seemed really to doubt whether she was welcome.

'You never know, do you?' The first shock over, Clarrie Piper was not conceding much. He gave a nod to the man with the tickets: 'That's all right, Sam. These two are on me.' Then he gave Vicky a nod: 'Come on in.'

The band started up. The noise was amplified beyond anything Laura or Vicky had heard before and bewildered by it, they paused just inside the hall. Knowing she could not be heard, Vicky turned to Laura and mouthed the word 'Grief!' They began to giggle, their nerves shocked by the volume of sound. Laura felt as though she had been struck by blast. It was sustained blast that seemed at first unbearable yet as it went on, they found it could be borne.

Clarrie had walked straight to the centre of the room thinking Vicky was behind him. When he turned and found she was still by the door, he came back frowning and took hold of her wrist. She went with him, laughing at his high-handed behaviour, and Laura was left forgotten. She was too exhilarated to care. If she wanted to dance, she could just go on to the floor and dance.

At the church dance, the couples had been comfortably spaced about the room. Here everyone was packed together. The music stopped occasionally, as though for breath, but there were no regular intervals. The dancing went on as though it were all one dance. Some of the dancers would break off and stand or wander about and dance again. People changed partners, shifting as they danced so their antics were performed in front of first one person, then another. The informality, the sense of freedom, filled Laura with joy. Here, she thought, there were no rivalries and possessive relationships, none of Camperlea's defensive evasion of life. Watching, she did not feel she was excluded; she was entertained.

The number of coloured people in the hall surprised her. Emigrants were rare visitors to Camperlea. They had scarcely been seen until they came in from Salthouse to shop. On the stage there were five boys – two had saxophones, two played electric guitars and a coloured boy was at the drums. One of the saxophone boys was singing. His singing could not be heard above the din, but sometimes he put his mouth to the microphone and screeched a word that struck the walls and split the air, but there was no telling what it was.

At last, intoxicated by uproar, Laura held out her hands towards a man in a check cotton jacket and began to sway and sing herself. He came over, laughing at her as though she were a joke, but she did not care about that. She shouted 'It's great' and he nodded agreement whether he heard or not. She danced wildly, feeling that here, in this classless, uncritical society, she had found some sort of escape. She was so excited that she laughed all the time and her partner, excited by her excitement. flung himself about in a physical fury, at times taking leaps into the air as though the dance itself were not enough to consume his energy. Their corybantics went on until, abruptly, the band came to a stop. Some of the dancers sat down where they had been dancing. In the lull the music seemed still to pulse in the air.

Laura asked: 'What dance was that?'
'What do you mean – what dance?'
'What is it called?'
'I don't know.'
'Was it the Frug?'
'Could be.'

117

Laura looked round for Vicky but Vicky was not in the hall. She said: 'Have you seen the girl I came with?'

'You mean that blonde bird? Piper's taken her off somewhere. Trust him. She's a real tomato. Beats me how he gets 'em.'

'What's your name?' Laura asked.

'Nick.'

'Nick what?'

'Just Nick.'

A crash startled the air. The dancers started up and Laura, impatient to begin again, leapt in to boisterous movement. Stimulated by her zeal, Nick threw himself about but in a moment a yellow-skinned man with black eyes and heavy mouth came edging towards her and thrust her partner out of the way. She was delighted to find she had been taken over and she told herself that Gilda had been right. A girl who had vivacity, could manage without beauty.

She watched this new partner, intending to smile and show she approved the change, but his eyes were half closed and he did not look at her. At times his eyes rolled up then shut again as though he were mesmerized. Laura had never before seen a man so sinuous, so dedicated to movement, so absorbed by the rhythm of his own body. He danced as though dancing were a ritual. While he danced, he held his hands up and shook them as though in an ecstatic transport.

Up on the stage the boy who was singing started to dance; then, from sheer exuberance, the boys with the guitars began jumping on the flimsy, shaking stage. Laura screamed with delight and shouted to her partner, but the yellow-skinned man could not hear and would not have heard if he could. Slowly but with concentrated purpose,

118

he shifted ground again, pushed aside another man, took over another girl.

Deciding to do some taking over herself, Laura looked round and saw a pair of red corduroy levis worn with a jacket of red and gold. There was magnificence. Dancing steadily towards the wearer, she caught his eye and grinned. He was as tall and as lean as a whippet. He grinned back and moved towards her.

Laura, with her tiny body, her spider-thin arms and legs, felt herself made for this activity. At dancing class, because she was small, she had had to take the feminine role but she had never enjoyed being steered round the room as though she did not know which way to go. Now, she felt, she had found the free world where all were equal and there was no nonsense about one leading and one being led.

The music stopped. She gazed in admiration at the young man in red and said: 'You're super.'

'You're not bad yourself,' he told her.

He had a long pale face that lacked the dazzle of his dress but he had a good-natured expression, the sort of expression, it seemed to Laura, on which might be built a mutual devotion. His name was Bert. This time she did not make the mistake of saying: 'Bert who?' Instead, she asked: 'Where do you come from?'

'Stepney.'

'Is that in London?'

'A-corse. Where d'you think?'

'Why did you come here? Wouldn't you rather be in London?'

He made a jeering noise and she realized that by questioning him in this way she was over-stepping convention. His evasiveness disconcerted her. It did not seem to belong to that home of open-natured generosity which was Laura's London. Afraid of saying the wrong thing, she kept silent, not knowing what to say, but it did not matter. Hardly anyone was talking. Here, it seemed, communication was by movement, not sound. The instinctive, animal atmosphere unnerved her, and she became conscious that she was without friends. She was the youngest in the room. The other girls had the confidence of being in their own milieu while she was alone among strangers. Although she danced with the men, she felt uncertain of them. She could not be sure that any one of them might not take leave of his senses and treat her as Clarrie Piper had treated her.

When she lost the impetus of first ardour, she realized how tired she was. Vivacity might stand in for beauty, but it was hard work. The man in red corduroy was wearing a wristwatch. She saw that it was nearly ten o'clock and began to worry about Vicky. What had happened to her? Supposing she had forgotten Laura and gone home without her?

Next time the music stopped, she said: 'I'll have to get back to Camperlea soon.'

Bert told her not to worry: 'There's a factory bus for the Camperlea girls.'

'When does it go?'

'Midnight.'

'Midnight! Grief! I have to be home by ten-thirty.'

'You kidding?'

'No, I'm not. My mother makes a fuss.'

'You don't have to worry about her.'

It was after ten when Vicky sauntered into the hall, serene, untouched, with Clarrie Piper glooming behind her. By then Laura had danced herself to a standstill. She ran to Vicky, saying: 'Can we go now?'

Vicky agreed. She smiled at Clarrie but said nothing. The two girls went to the cloakroom where other girls, Salthouse girls, were chatting in a group. The chatting stopped when Vicky entered.

As she gazed, innocent-eyed, at her image in the glass, the other girls gave her sidelong glances. They were forced to admire her but it was a resentful admiration. She did not belong here. Why did she come here to steal their men?

Unaware of their hostility, Vicky examined herself critically and banged a puff over her nose then she looked round at the other girls, smiling so gently they had to respond, but their smiles were brief and unencouraging.

Clarrie was waiting in the entrance. As Vicky came out, he was watching the cloakroom door and he stepped forward to claim her. She said: 'We must go.'

'Not yet, you mustn't. I want a word.' He pulled her away from Laura who saw that the darkness outside was complete. It could be later than she realized. Vicky and Clarrie were talking in voices too low to be heard but Laura could imagine their conversation to be the same sort of desultory to and fro that had held them at the church gate. It need never be concluded and Laura, knowing herself forgotten, crossed over and stood at Vicky's elbow. When Vicky looked her way, she said: 'I'm sorry, but I'll be in terrible trouble if I don't get home soon.'

Clarrie Piper looked at her with disgust but Vicky said: 'She has to get back. She's only a kid, you know.'

'Right.' Clarrie led them to the parking lot and when Vicky went to the motor-bicycle, he pushed in front of her, saying: 'I'll get you there all right.'

'But how will you return?'

'There's a bus, isn't there?'

With Vicky on the pillion and Laura on the tank, Clarrie ran the machine down to the road and took off with the assurance of a professional.

When in the saddle, careless and inexperienced, Vicky depended for safety on the consideration accorded her good looks, her laughter and her sex. If she touched fifty, she and her passenger credited themselves with extreme daring; but to Clarrie fifty was a mere beginning. They were probably doing seventy before they reached the level crossing. As the front wheel hit the rail, the bicycle jumped and Laura, thrown forward, struck the handle-bars with her brow. Pressing her head down between her knuckles, she repeated, like an incantation against danger: 'Please don't go so fast ... don't go so fast ... don't go so fast', but no one heard her and Clarrie would not have heeded had he heard. They seemed to take the bridge at a leap, then they gathered speed on the long road to the roundabout. There they swerved into Camperlea without slowing down and went with noisy fury down the shuttered, empty High Street. When Clarrie made his expert stop at the top of Rowantree Avenue, Laura was too stunned to move.

'Get off, you,' Clarrie shoved her shoulder and pulling herself together, she slid off the tank and tried to adopt a breezy air of composure.

'Grief,' she said, 'you must have been doing a ton.'

Clarrie ignored her. He looked round at Vicky and asked: 'Which way for you?'

'This will do for me, too,' Vicky got off the pillion and waited for the B.S.A. to be handed over. Clarrie remained in the saddle.

'You far to go?' he asked.

'Not far.'

'Where do you live?'

Vicky vaguely indicated the hinterland round Rowan-tree Avenue and said: 'Over there somewhere.'

'Get on. I'll run you to the door.'

'No. I'd rather go alone.'

'I get it. Scared of your old man, eh?' Clarrie spoke mockingly yet he was not displeased and he was grinning as he got off the machine and let her take it. Seated, she looked round to where Laura waited, protective to the last, and said: 'Tea on Monday?'

'Yes, super.'

As Vicky made off, Clarrie shouted: 'See you next week, eh?' She did not reply and in a moment the curve of the High Street hid her from view.

Free to go now, Laura ran down the avenue, pausing once to look back. Clarrie still stood at the end of the road, staring after Vicky as though by staring he could penetrate bricks and mortar and see which way she had gone.

Reaching home, Laura glanced fearfully at the front room window where her mother sometimes stood in the dark, waiting to pounce on a latecomer. Laura, fortunately, was not late enough to merit such an attack.

Mrs Fletcher, in the sitting-room mending her husband's winter vests, said sternly. 'About time, my girl,' but her heart was not in it. Something had distracted her from the clock. Or, maybe, she had been misled by the fact Mr Fletcher was still in the yard, sluicing and brushing the flagstones by the light that fell through the conservatory glass.

She let Laura settle to her milk and biscuits, then said: 'The sales start on Monday.'

Laura murmured, pretending interest, but her mind was elsewhere. Her mother's laxity seemed to her all part of her expanding life. Even Mrs Fletcher must realize that her daughter was growing up. The room that so long had been her centre of reality now seemed to Laura to have lost substance. With its out-of-date furnishings, its aura of frustration and complaint, it had become meaningless to her. Reality was now an ante-room to romance, a crowded hall noisy with music and full of young men who said: 'You're not bad yourself.' Bemused by her triumphs, Laura heard her mother talking as from another world:

'Your father could do with some new underpants. And these vests are getting pretty thin. We'll take the bus down to Peckham's and see what there is in the men's department.'

'But not on Monday?'

'Yes. The first day's always the best.'

'I'm going to tea with Vicky Logan.'

Mrs Fletcher said nothing but bent over her work with mouth firmly shut. Laura, dragged away from her joyous reflections, watched apprehensively, knowing that this sunken posture, this set mouth, denoted anger of the most bitter kind.

Out in the conservatory, Mr Fletcher was knocking the water off his gum-boots. Tired, content, happy in his oldest clothes, he appeared in the doorway and was met by his wife's rage:

'Don't bring those boots in here.'

Startled, he looked at Laura to see what the trouble was. Laura, defiant but miserable, looked back. He said nothing but, propping himself against the jamb of the door, he worked off one boot on the toe of the other. When they were both off, he picked them up, one at a time, and stared into each.

He was always slow to enter a battlefield and at last

Mrs Fletcher could contain herself no longer. 'Come in here,' she ordered him. 'What do you think? I asked that girl to come to Peckham's on Monday and she wants to have tea with Vicky Logan instead.'

'All right. All right,' Laura mumbled, 'I'll go to the grotty sales.'

Such half-hearted surrender would not pacify Mrs Fletcher. She said with great firmness: 'That Vicky Logan is doing her no good. She's too old for Laura; and we all know what the Logans are like. Never ... never did I think the day would come when my daughter would put a stranger before her own mother.'

Mr Fletcher, gazing into the second gum-boot, made a non-committal noise.

'Put that boot down,' said his wife. 'You are her father. It's your duty to speak to her.'

Mr Fletcher dropped the boot and entering the room in his socks, looked at Laura with sad, pleading eyes: 'You mustn't be selfish, Lory. Your mother has done a lot for you. Now you're growing up, you must do something for her.'

'Daddy, I said I'd go to Peckham's on Monday. Isn't that enough?'

Of course it was not enough; or anything like enough. Mrs Fletcher began to splash about in a welter of past wrongs. In a lifetime of sacrifices made on her behalf, Laura had done nothing right.

'When she's dependent on the strangers,' said Mrs Fletcher grimly, 'she'll see what they'll do for her. Take that woman Button, for instance! What did she do for them when she got them over there? And what did this girl say to me? When I said they didn't get the food they got at home, this girl said: "Oh, yes, we did. We got shepherd's pie!" She contradicted me – *me*, who'd sent Mrs Button ten pounds out of my post office book!'

Laura caught her father's eye and they exchanged a desolate glance. She wondered if Tom, in bed in the room above, was listening and thanking his stars that he was safely out of trouble.

'And now she's picked up with Vicky Logan. It's Vicky Logan this and Vicky Logan that. I'd just like to know what Vicky Logan has done for her?'

She lent me a handkerchief, Laura said to herself. It was unfair, of course, that Vicky should earn more gratitude for that one act than went to Mrs Fletcher with all her deserving; yet, there it was! One's feelings were what they were. No one could change them.

'Very well,' said Mrs Fletcher in threatening tone. 'Go, my girl. Go to the Logans'! But if anything happens, don't blame me.'

Laura could bear no more. 'What could happen?' She jumped up in disgust: 'Really, Mummy, you're impossible!'

'Impossible, am I! You wait, my girl. You have a lot to learn.'

'*Im*-possible.' Leaving the room and slamming the door after her, Laura had the satisfaction of cutting off her mother in mid-sentence.

Sunday was a tense day, ending in compromise. They would go early to the sales in South Camperlea and Laura would later proceed to Flamingo Park. The shopping done, Laura walked with her mother to the bus stop and was about to go on when Mrs Fletcher said:

'So you're going to the Logans'?' She had, it seemed, persuaded herself that Laura would repent and return with her to Rowantree Avenue.

Fearing that even now some piece of emotional trickery would hold her, Laura said 'I won't be late' and ran before more could be said.

'Ah, here's Laura now,' said Mrs Logan, comfortable in her sun-filled alcove. 'You're just in time. The tea's made. Sit here beside me. There, how nice!'

How nice! How nice! echoed in Laura's head. How nice this household where everyone was kind! How charming Mrs Logan was! And considerate! Her eyes would linger on Vicky, her adored, lovely child, yet from sheer generosity she would turn to include Laura, gathering her in to share the affection between them. Laura could have sat all evening delighting in Mrs Logan, but Vicky had different ideas.

As soon as tea was over, she said: 'Mummy says there's a new shop in the Grove. It's just opened. She says it's "with it".' Vicky smiled at this worn-out phrase which had recently come into her mother's vocabulary.

Mrs Logan laughed, happy to feel on equal terms with the girls. 'It's called The Boutique,' she said. 'And what do you think! The windows are painted all over with flowers. You can't see in.'

Astounded, Laura breathed: 'How super!'

'Let's go and look at it,' Vicky said.

'You mean now?'

Vicky nodded. Her expression was pure and direct but a flicker of one eye told Laura that they must get away from Mrs Logan. Laura could only agree.

'You don't mind, Mummy, do you?'

Mrs Logan looked crestfallen that the fun must end but

she said: 'Don't worry about me. You girls have things to talk about.'

And indeed they had. On the esplanade, private among the holiday-makers, Vicky said: 'Laura, I want you to promise not to tell Clarrie Piper where I live.'

'You don't really think I'd tell him?'

'He might try and get it out of you.'

'He can try but he won't succeed. Just think what your father would say!'

'What, lazycow Herbie!' Vicky put her head back and laughed, then seeing that Laura was pained, added in palliating confidence: 'It's Mummy I'm thinking about. She had a breakdown after Ronnie was killed. She's always liable to . . . to be ill again.'

'I knew you had to stay home for weeks.'

'She couldn't be left alone. One of us had to be there. She wouldn't believe Ronnie was dead. If you left her for a minute, she'd begin talking to him. I heard her once in the next room. She was saying: "You know, Ronnie darling, they're trying to make me believe you're dead but I know better." It was weird.'

'I can imagine.'

'This is in confidence, of course. She's all right now but you never know. Any shock and she might collapse again. You do understand, don't you?'

Fervent in sympathy, Laura said: 'Oh, I do. I *do*.'

At the corner of the Grove they met a red-haired girl, sumptuously dressed, who smiled sadly on Vicky as she passed and left behind her a scent of gardenias.

'One of Ronnie's girls,' Vicky whispered.

Laura stared round in jealous surprise: 'Did he have girl friends?'

'What do you think?'

128

'Your mother said he wanted no one but her.'

Vicky gave a laugh and murmured: 'Poor old mum!'

Laura had expected to hear more about Clarrie Piper and having been told nothing, she asked: 'Where did you and Clarrie go when you left the dance?'

'Oh, not far. We wandered around and then we stood in the car park and talked a bit.'

'Didn't he want to dance?'

Vicky laughed: 'There were other things he wanted to do more.'

'Did you have to fight him off?'

'More or less. I had to let him know that he couldn't take anything for granted.'

'Grief, yes.' Laura glanced sideways at Vicky, puzzled by Vicky's smiling face. 'Do you really like him?' she asked.

'No. I don't think so.'

The Boutique was a disappointment. Though the windows were painted all over with flowers, the dim interior had nothing to show but dresses that were little different from the dresses in Peckham's sale. There was a display of plastic jewellery.

Vicky bent to the little looking-glass and held earrings against her ears. The earrings were bunches of transparent discs, brilliantly green, flimsy as gauze. She screwed them on and turned for Laura's approval. She held back her head, her throat curving as whitely as a swan's, and shook her head so the discs glimmered like water-globules through the fair-silvery silk of her hair.

'How do I look?'

'Beyond dreams.'

Vicky laughed and went to the counter at the back of the shop. When she returned, she was carrying two small paper bags, the paper, like the windows, covered all over with flowers. She gave one to Laura.

'For me?'

'We'll wear them next Saturday,' Vicky said.

Going home on the bus, Vicky took her earrings from their bag. They were pink instead of green. She held one up and the thin pink discs shimmered and moved and tinkled with the movement of the bus.

Now, Laura felt, she knew what friendship was. She had had friends before but they were the sort of friends one made when nothing better was offered: not loved, simply not unloved. They had saved her from utter solitude but she did not trust them.

This friendship had nobility. Laura felt her own nature deepened and widened by it. Were she asked to die for Vicky she would, she decided, die. At least, she would give the proposition serious thought.

Seeing Laura on Saturday in her glitter earrings and her no longer very golden dress, Mrs Fletcher frowned: 'You're too young to be going out, dressed up, night after night.'

'I don't go night after night. We go once a week. You don't want me to be in every night, do you?'

Mrs Fletcher would have liked to say 'Yes' but instead asked anxiously: 'What sort of young men do you meet at these dances?'

'They're all right.'

'I hope they're nice boys. Mrs Vosper says the vicar of St Barnabas' is a good man. But don't forget now, Laura! If any young man says anything you don't like, turn on your heel and walk away. Don't argue with him. Just have nothing more to do with him.'

Mrs Fletcher was never explicit and Laura asked with an air of innocence: 'What sort of things?'

Her mother gave her a straight look: 'Why do you ask? You're always telling me you know everything.'

Laura was defeated, and knew it. As she took herself off, she grumbled about being delayed. Here she was with life and its problems ahead of her, and all her mother could do was hold her up with vague admonitions and pointless fears. She was going down to Flamingo Park. Vicky had offered to pick her up at the end of her road but if this happened every week, sooner or later some busybody would say to Mrs Fletcher: 'I saw your Laura getting on to a motor-cycle at the end of the road.' Then the trouble would start. Apart from that, Laura longed for Flamingo Park. The Logans' house was a joy to her. She wanted to see Mrs Logan. She waited to see Mr Logan. And this time she would be prepared for him.

She now knew Mr Logan was a deceiver; an habitual deceiver. At first, she had seen his embrace as a spontaneous expression of feeling. Now she feared it was not. But even if it were, Mrs Logan was none the less deceived. And Laura had responded willingly. She had seen herself rushing headlong into a grown-up situation. Then, with no more than a kiss on the credit side of Experience, she had come up against poor deluded Mrs Logan.

At first she had tried to tell herself that middle-aged women had all the best men, but it was no good. She knew she had to give up Mr Logan. It was a tragic situation and one that called for finesse. She consulted several library novels in which girls were forced to give up the men they loved and she had hit upon a likely rebuke: 'I love you,

131

too, Lord Basingstoke, but we have to think of Lady Basingstoke.'

'I love you, too, Mr Logan, but we have to think of Mrs Logan.' She was ready for him. She had only to await her opportunity.

Released from her mother and the impatience engendered by her mother, Laura hurried down Rowantree Avenue. She felt could she lift both feet from the pavement, she would fly up into the air. She imagined herself catapulted to Flamingo Park by the sheer force of her desire to be there; yet the ground held to her. For all her gaiety, she could only run. Seeing the bus crossing the end of the road, she ran so swiftly that as it left the stop, she leapt like a moufflon on to the step. The bus, too, was in a hurry. No bus had ever been nearer to Laura's heart. At stops, it barely paused before the bell pinged and it was in flight again. Down, down, down to the sea. Down to Flamingo Park.

Mrs Logan was in her usual seat. Vicky had just finished dressing. As she entered, Laura caught her breath, amazed that Vicky's beauty could be made more beautiful by her green earrings and the green sequins which she had stuck on her eyelids. The sequins lay in a row above the lashes so that they threw off green fire with every movement of her head. And she had a new dress of green silk. All this green, shimmering and catching the golden light, made her powdery flesh more white, her hair more fair.

Laura said: 'I've never seen anyone more lovely.'

'*Isn't* she lovely!' Mrs Logan's voice broke on the words. This time she could not take her eyes off Vicky. Laura was quite forgot.

Vicky laughed at their admiration and said: 'Let's go.'

132

Mrs Logan pleaded: 'Don't go on the motor-cycle, darling. The wind will ruin your hair.'

'Don't worry. I've a little brush in my bag.'

'Oh dear,' Mrs Logan looked at Laura as though Laura could help her. 'I do hate that motor-bicycle.'

'Silly pet. We'll be all right.'

Clarrie was standing on the kerb in front of the Salthouse hall. He waved Vicky down before she could turn into the parking lot and giving no preliminary greeting, said: 'Get off.'

Laura left the pillion and Vicky, meekly obedient, let Clarrie Piper take the bicycle from her. Seating himself in the saddle, he bent in a covetous way over the engine and said: 'Wouldn't mind having one like it.'

'Have you ever had a bike of your own?'

'Yah. Had a Honda when I was a kid. Smashed it on the North Circular. Had three cars different times. Last one was a write-off. I'll have another when I've got a bit in hand.'

'Wasn't the car insured?'

Clarrie, hanging over the machine, muttered about 'trouble' but he did not say what the trouble was. He raised his head at last: 'I like these old bikes. I like the weight of them. Come on. Let's run 'er round a bit.'

'What about Laura?' Vicky said.

'It's dodgy with 'er on the tank. She'll be all right here. Tell 'er to go in. We won't be long.'

'It's not much fun for her going in alone. She doesn't know anyone.' He kicked the starter as though he had not heard and sat listening to the engine with an absorbed expression, then suddenly he said: 'She better get on, then.'

Laura took her old perch on the tank and bent down into an aroma of engine oil. They set off slowly towards the downs. Clarrie, it seemed, was uncertain where to go. He was wearing his shirt open at the neck with sleeves rolled up. Glancing at his arms stretched on either side of her, Laura saw they were brown and thickly muscled, with a matt of black hair from wrist to elbow. He had on ordinary grey flannel trousers. There was, Laura thought, no interest or imagination about his dress, nothing to denote the fashion of a new age. Through the fumes of oil and petrol, she could catch the smell of his armpits. She sensed in a detached way, his masculine attraction but liked him none the better for it.

They reached the lane where Mr Fletcher had taken Tom and Laura for Sunday walks. Clarrie slowed to a pause and put his feet down. 'Where's this go, then?' Vicky did not know. Laura, who did know, felt, for no reason she could recall, an acute unwillingness to visit the lane again.

'There's nothing down there,' she said; 'it only leads to the Creek,' but Clarrie took no notice of her.

He dragged the front wheel round and the machine bumped and bounced them along the rough track between abandoned allotments and the flat dispiriting turnip field. No one worked the land now. It had been sold for development and soon the factories and houses would spread and cover it.

In the old days, when it had been country, unusual flowers could be found here, but now the urban grime was killing everything. Only dandelions, groundsel, white convolvulus and coarse grass bordered the track. People had dumped mattresses in the field and hillocks of old tin cans. The whole place was like some big untidy backyard.

The sky had misted over and there was something disturbing about the white, refracted light. Although it was

Saturday, the day dedicated to pleasure, Laura expected to hear the bells of Salthouse church. Remembering the insistent bell-beating frustrations of childhood, she remembered the last time she had been down the lane and suddenly knew why she had been unwilling to return.

It was three years before, when Camperlea people still came out on the bus to walk in their Sunday clothes. Laura, alone for some reason, had come upon a group of people standing about a small white object on the ground. When she got nearer she saw the object was a puppy. The puppy was unconscious but shivering violently and the stout woman who stood over it, wailed: 'This keeps happening. I can't take any more of it. I'd finish the poor thing off if I could.'

A young man spoke up briskly: 'I'd do it. Give me a brick and I'd finish it in a jiffy.'

Laura wanted to cry 'Don't kill it' but she dared not speak in front of all those grown-up people. For all she knew, the right thing might be to put the animal out of its misery. The young man had gone to the brickfield and seeing him coming back with his weapon, Laura had run away. Mrs Fletcher, who loved dogs, cried out indignantly when she heard this story: 'It was only a puppy fit. They often have them. The little thing would have got over them if they'd let it live.'

The lane had looked bleak enough in the livid light; now it looked bleaker as Laura saw it in the light of her remembered cowardice. She felt as though it had been her task to save the dog; and she had failed.

'What's this?' said Clarrie, slowing down to stare at the brickworks' chimney.

'They used to make bricks here,' Laura said. Her father told her that tramps who slept against the brick kiln for warmth were found dead in the morning. Though the kiln had been cold for years, the Fletcher children had seen it as sinister and they would dare each other to go near it. Beyond the brickfield were the clay pits: a region of artificial hills and ponds where rats ran about and Laura had once fallen into the water when trying to reach some bullrushes.

Mr Fletcher said that long ago there had been a country house beside the Creek. The house had been pulled down but part of the garden wall remained and there were two cottages where the outdoor servants had lived. Sometimes he was too tired to go farther than the cottages but when he had the energy, he would take them as far as the hangar which was built out into the creek. The hangar was always the ultimate point of a walk. At the Creek the track turned north and ran up through dull country to join the main road above.

These walks had been a delight to the children. Their father, who kept in the background at home, used to talk all the time, treating of some splendid subject such as the nature of the stars or the Navy or the places he had seen abroad. He showed them that the world was wide and full of marvels and one event led to another. He told them that the Salthouse land had been bought by speculators and one day it would all be built over. Even the Creek, he said, would be drained and built over. These projects had seemed to the children visionary in the extreme, yet he had been right about the Salthouse land. No one ever came here from Camperlea now. The Sunday playground had changed into a town and become the preserve of strangers.

After the ruined cottages there was the long run down to the Creek.

'What's that, then?' said Clarrie Piper, as the hangar appeared black in the distance.

'It's a hangar,' Laura said.

'A what?'

'There used to be sea-planes on the Creek and that's where they were serviced. The Navy left a lot of stuff behind.'

'Hah!' Clarrie put on speed as though imagining he might find something of value at the hangar.

The track turned and twisted, passing through an ancient orchard. The trees were bare of leaves, fruitless, distorted, grey-green with lichen and all bent towards the north as though a killer wind had swept over them and left behind nothing but phosphorescent corpses. There was a mile or more of this tree cemetery before the sea-wall came in sight. It was high tide and the water had spread up among the reeds and the coarse grasses that tufted the edge of the downs.

Clarrie stopped opposite the hangar and propped up the B.S.A. They leant against the wall and surveyed the Creek that, shallow and unnavigable by anything bigger than a row-boat, looked now like a great waterway separating Camperlea from Salthouse. There was one little island. It had a hut from which, Mr Fletcher said, the excise men used to watch for smugglers.

Vicky had never been here before and she was astonished by the extent of the Creek and the desolation surrounding it. Clarrie looked at the hangar, his expression spiteful and calculating as though he disliked the big black structure and was wondering how to get the better of it.

After several minutes of resentful contemplation, he turned and, standing with his back to the wall, said:

'Snout?' – he held out a crumpled packet of cigarettes.

Vicky took one but Laura said: 'I don't smoke.' She hoped this assertion would rouse Clarrie's surprise but Clarrie was indifferent to Laura and everything to do with Laura.

He drew on his cigarette and swallowed the smoke, his white face set blankly. She thought that nothing about him was interesting. His trousers had an old-fashioned cuff. His shirt, a cheap-looking affair, had shadow stripes. He could have been any Camperlea workman.

She said: 'Have you ever been to Chelsea?'

'Yeh.'

'What happens there?'

'Nothing.'

'Nothing?'

'Just rich kids, dressed up, walking round thinking people're looking at them.'

'Well, that's something. I've seen pictures. They look super.'

Clarrie shrugged. When he said nothing more, Laura asked: 'Do you take pot?'

'Pot!' Clarrie's mouth twisted in disgust. 'A kid like you talking about pot!' He turned away and speaking directly to Vicky as though she and he were adults in the company of a child, said: 'I don't hold with chicks trying to be clever. I don't go for that groovy lark. Lot'a pouffy kids showing off. I like it real. I got ideas. I want to do things.'

'What sort of things?' Vicky watched him with sympathy.

'I want to be something. Might become a commercial. Need a car, though. Once I get the down payment, might get a Rapier.'

Vicky said: 'You can get a Mini for about a hundred down. Or you could get one second-hand.'

'Don't want a Mini. I like big cars. Don't want a used car. I'm not buying other people's trouble. I like things fresh and new.' He looked Vicky up and down, his eyes avid, and his face took on a satisfied expression. He seemed to see some especial virtue in knowing what he wanted and wanting what he did want. Laura, having been crushed into silence, thought that Clarrie was not merely dull, he was a man without resonance: a bore and a boor.

Suddenly he threw down his cigarette, trod it out with a decisive movement and turned again to the hangar. He said, 'Let's see, then,' and swung himself over the wall. He began to cross the grass with a sauntering swagger but the ground was sea marsh and his feet sank into mud. Unable to maintain the swagger, he began to make antic movements for Vicky's entertainment.

'What's inside?' he shouted.

Vicky did not know. Laura was not saying.

The hangar, being a naval artifact, had been built to last. At the top, where roof joined sides, the wind had pulled the canvas from the struts, but the building was sound. It had a formidable air as though, standing there for thirty solitary years, it had acquired a place in the world and its own reason for existence. Laura felt, as she had felt in childhood, that the great black blank face was keeping a watch on them and their intrusion must not go too far.

Clarrie went round to the right. The girls did not try to follow him but they knew he expected to be watched. When he reached the water's edge, he stared down at the muddy bottom, then he bent his knees as though about to lower himself in at the water's edge.

Laura shouted: 'The mud's very soft.' Whether he heard her or not, he gave up the idea of wading to the front of the hangar and crossed to the side where there was a ledge just under the water surface. With his hands pressed to the canvas, he stretched out a foot but he could not reach the ledge. He risked falling in and this time Vicky shouted: 'Oh, Clarrie, don't.'

Laura told her: 'He doesn't need to go in the front. There's a door on the other side.' Before Vicky could call out again, he suddenly stepped back from the hangar, stared at it, then, making a rush at it, threw himself upon the fabric and began beating on it with his hands. The fabric held. Knowing no other way in, he was trying to break through the side and seemed distraught that he could not do so. When he could make no impression with his fists, he began kicking at the fabric with his feet. The girls could hear him screaming in fury as he banged and kicked in a performance so futile, it looked insane.

'Shall I tell him about the entrance?'

Vicky was observing Clarrie with a strange smile and said: 'I don't think I would if I were you.' Laura, disturbed by both of them, moved away. A few yards to the left there was a gap in the wall and she was able to reach the hangar over a flint ridge which formed a path to the door. She knew the door well. If it were not held open, it fell shut and one had to feel one's way through semi-darkness to the platform at the back of the hangar.

She knew the way to the platform. Standing on it, she could see out through the end of the hangar which was open to the Creek. Not much light came in even on a fine day. Now it was scarcely possible to make out the cat-walks that ran along on either side. A glint came from the floor which was under water at high tide so the hangar became a dock and the planes could be floated in for servicing.

Laura looked out on a view of the Camperlea gas-works on the far side of the Creek: a scene as dismal as a steel engraving, framed by the mourning blackness of the hangar's edge.

This prospect had been the final event for the Fletcher children in the ever eventful walk down the lane. Looking down on the in-washing sea, she remembered how she and Tom had planned to turn the hangar into a theatre. The platform was as wide as a stage. They would write their own plays, of course, and produce them so splendidly that the whole of Camperlea would come to see them. The lane would be alive with cars and buses and pedestrians. Walking home, they discussed with their father the problems of lighting the stage and seating the audience. He treated the project seriously and seriously answered all their questions. Tom thought people could come by boat, rowing into the hangar on one tide and rowing out on the next. Between tides they would sit in the boats to watch the play. He was disconcerted to learn that the interval between tides was nearly twelve and a half hours.

'We could serve refreshments before they left,' he said.

Had Mrs Fletcher been there she would have dismissed the whole idea as ridiculous but their father let them talk, knowing that time would defeat their designs just as it had defeated his own.

No sound came from outside the hangar. Clarrie must have given up his attempt to batter it down. The door opened; an arrow of light fell towards the platform, and Vicky called: 'Come on, Laura. We're going back to the dance.'

Clarrie, his face sullen was already on the saddle. He started off before Laura had properly got a grip on the centre of the handle-bar. She was thrown to one side as he turned and was forced, unwillingly, to hold to his arm. He went back at angry speed, with the tyres bouncing and thudding on the broken ground.

When he stopped outside the hall, the girls dismounted but Clarrie, still pale and sullen, jerked his head at the entrance and said to Vicky: 'You don't want to go in there?'

'Yes. After all, we did come to dance.'

Clarrie's manner did not change but he seemed aware that he had made a fool of himself and Vicky was no longer compliant. He looked down at the engine, mumbling: 'Had enough of that scene.' He looked up from under his brows and pleaded with a frown: 'I'll put the bike in. You come with me. We'll talk it over.'

'Later, perhaps. Laura wants to dance. I'm going in with her.'

'Right,' he sounded humble enough. 'See you in half an hour, then?'

Vicky nodded and went with Laura into the hall. The band was making its usual din and Vicky, laughing, caught Laura's hand and pulled her on to the floor. At once one of the men moved over between the girls and facing Vicky, adjusted his movements to hers. Laura stepped back to the edge of the room and watched Vicky, who, with sleepy smiling face, swayed in a mere token effort that at times slackened to nothing but a languorous roll of the hips. And why need she do more? She had only to be there and one by one the men came edging towards her, each offering himself when his chance came, knowing his chances were slight.

The music stopped and Bert joined Laura to ask: 'Where's Piper, then?'

'He didn't want to come in.'

'Silly nit. What's he think he'll get? The going-steady lark?'

'I don't know.'

'She's no easy chick. There's nothing in it for him.' The drums began again: 'Want to dance?' Grinning, Bert began jerking and leaping, expecting the same from Laura.

An hour passed before Vicky left the floor and joined Laura who asked: 'Aren't you going out to see Clarrie?' It was nearly time to go home.

Vicky took a hand-mirror from her bag and staring into it, said vaguely: 'I don't want to see him.' She sighed as though Clarrie were a problem she had not the energy to face.

Laura wished she could ask: 'Is it all over? Are we really rid of him?' longing for confidences and the assurance that Clarrie would trouble them no more; but Vicky said nothing. She seemed so little concerned about Clarrie, she would not even speak of him.

'Do you think we could go now?' Vicky asked.

'Yes, lets.'

Outside, Vicky appeared not to notice Clarrie Piper standing in the car park where he had probably been standing for the last hour and a half.

Laura whispered: 'There's Clarrie.'

'Oh!' Vicky's cool tone was a reprimand. She saw no cause to be nervous of Clarrie but as she made to pass him, murmuring 'Good-night', he snatched rapidly at her and held her as fiercely as he had once held Laura.

'What's the game, then?'

'No game.' Vicky spoke quietly and reasonably: 'I told you we came here to dance.'

'You told me. Right. I 'eard you. You said 'arf 'n' hour What is it, then? Sort'a cat and mouse game, eh?' Clarrie was trembling. Each word came venomously, like an insult: 'I'm not standing for it.'

'No?' Vicky smiled at his presumption and Laura, admiring, wondered if Vicky's pleasure in Clarrie resulted from her power over him. Was Vicky gratified by the sight of Clarrie shaking, literally shaking, with desirous anger? Perhaps not. Perhaps she did not care one way or the other. She laughed and Clarrie struck her across the face.

Laura gasped in horror but Vicky, who had almost been thrown off balance, retrieved herself without a word. She kept her eyes fixed on Clarrie. Half her face was in shadow, the other half, lit by the street lighting, looked mild and trustful as though she had received not a blow but an offer of protective love.

'That's wiped the smile off your face,' said Clarrie, watching her with sly and bitter relish. He lifted his hand again and Laura shouted: 'Leave her alone. Let her go.' Clarrie snorted his contempt and Laura, the more furious at being despised, said: 'If you don't leave her alone I'll get Bert. I'll get all the men. I'll get the factory foreman.'

'The fucking foreman!' Clarrie muttered but he dropped his hold on Vicky who, with nothing to keep her there, remained beside him.

'Come on.' Laura now laid hold on her and shook her: 'It's late. If I keep going home late, my mother won't let me come again.'

Vicky murmured 'All right', and let Laura lead her to the motor-bicycle. She pushed it down to the road where Laura saw, in the light from the street lamps, that Vicky's cheek was dark from the blow but her expression was almost exalted. It seemed that something had come to her like a revelation. The bliss of martyrdom, perhaps. Such bliss was not to Laura's taste.

Clarrie, back in the darkness, watched their departure. He made no move to stop them but it was not until they crossed the railway-line that Laura felt they were safe from him.

Paused at Rowantree Avenue, Vicky had lost her exalted look. She hung over the handle-bars as though weighed down by weariness and depression and she gave no parting invitation to Laura.

'You won't go again, will you?' Laura asked.

'I suppose not.'

So that was the end of Clarrie! Laura would not have to deceive her mother again. Relieved, and exhausted after her anger with Clarrie, she put her hands on Vicky's arm and burst out: 'Oh, Vicky!' but Vicky was not responsive.

'We'll talk about it another time,' she said as she kicked the starter and she was gone before Laura could ask: 'When?'

Having suffered through the doldrums of Sunday, Laura went on Monday to telephone Vicky. Seeing her go, Mrs Fletcher pointed to the plastic bag that contained the week's washing: 'Don't forget this,' she said and Laura snatched it up.

Once the clothes were moving in the machine, she ran to the telephone-box, certain that Vicky would want to see her that very afternoon; but Vicky's voice was vague and discouraging. She said sadly: 'Mummy's not too well.'

'When will I see you?' Laura asked.

'I'll send you a card.'

Laura, knowing herself dismissed, pretended cheerfulness and brightly said: 'Oh, yes, do.'

Had Vicky no use for her now? Wandering back to the launderette, she wondered if Saturday's incident had meant not only the end of Clarrie but the end of her friendship with Vicky. At the thought of returning to the eventless era of pre-Vicky days, she felt she could scarcely bear to live. She certainly could not live in Camperlea.

London, almost forgotten during the last weeks, began again to glitter in her fancy. If she could not go to Flamingo Park, she could go to Mr Logan's reading room, there to view the London scene in *Vogue* and *Harper's Bazaar*.

She went to the reading room at three o'clock, but the periodicals were not available. An old man, dilapidated and unnaturally thin, had fallen asleep across one of them. A woman had weighed the other down with a string bag full of boxes. Sitting beside the woman and in front of the man, Laura waited for one or other to make a move. The man was sodden with the nectar of oblivion; he would not wake in a hurry. The woman was a Camperlea character who wore the same clothes winter and summer and talked aloud to herself in the streets. Now it was mid-summer with the city damp beneath the heat-fog of the sky and there she was pinned into her bottle-green coat, three or four old woollen cardigans showing at the neck. Her life was spent in walking from North to South Camperlea and back again. Whenever she reached a kerb, she stopped and loudly counted a hundred before crossing the road. Mr Fletcher could remember when she had been a pretty, well-dressed girl living near the seafront in a basement flat. During the war, a bomb had brought the house down on top of her and she had been trapped for nearly a week before she was found. 'She went off her rocker, poor thing,' he said; and off her rocker she still was.

'I wonder if you have finished with *Vogue*?' Laura asked politely and the woman, shooting round in alarm, seized on the magazine and held to it, giving Laura a sullen squinny that forced her to retreat. The woman smoothed the cover of the magazine, pressed the bag more firmly down on it, and began to deal with the boxes. She pulled out half a dozen from the top then looked with anxious suspicion on those below. One, apparently, was recalcitrant. She brought it out, muttering her annoyance, and began to untie it. It was a small lozenge box so covered with string as to be almost invisible. Muttering, hissing and clicking her tongue, she worked on the knots and at last got them all untied. Holding the box naked in one hand, she began with the other to sort out the cords that had come from it. Having laid them in order, she was about to replace them when the box slipped, fell and opened on the floor. It was empty. With a threatening growl, the woman darted after it, retrieved it, tied it up again – a slow business – and stowed it away. She replaced all the boxes, drew the bag strings and started to shuffle in her seat.

'She's going, she's going,' Laura gleefully thought but instead the woman paused and groaned. Some new and fearful demand had been made upon her. She sat for some minutes, eyes closed as though in prayer, then, sighing and grumbling, faced the task ahead. She began to unpack all the boxes.

Laura gave up, thinking: 'If I stayed in Camperlea, I'd become like that,' and she went to the library.

In the old days, before she was taken up by girls like Vicky and Gilda, Laura had tried to enter the library unobserved. No girl in Camperlea had anything to gain by an addiction to serious reading. When Laura took *The Times Literary Supplement* to school, Gilda had scornfully said: 'Men don't like girls who read papers like that,' and it was true of Camperlea men, if of no others. Yet the library, a dark toast-rack of battered, grimy books, had once been Laura's refuge and the fostress of her early imaginings.

Now she had safely skirted a reputation for eccentricity and with Vicky as Best Friend, she felt she could do very much as she liked.

There had been plans to modernize the library at one time. The *Evening Herald* had advocated new bindings, new shelving and lighter reading matter, but later had to deplore the fact that all the money had gone 'down the reading room drain'. The library remained as it always had been, with 'Carnegie Library' carved in yellow stonework over the entrance. The shelves were congested and some of the books were so old, they might be valuable. In some corners the lights had to burn all day and Laura, crab-walking down the alleys, used to dream of coming on someone as handsome as Dick Garside but with a taste for Dostoievski. No such person, of course, was to be found in Camperlea. Only the most dismal young men came to the public library. They all looked like Hen Clarke: thin and stooped, glasses slipping down long, damp noses, limp bodies hung with raincoats of no known colour. Hen was the worst of them because he could not be ignored. When Laura met him, he bestowed upon her smiles of melting awfulness.

Laura and Hen had first met at the christening font. Mr Fletcher, as one might expect, had made up to Mrs Clarke, asking her 'What's the baby's name?' Being told 'Henry', Mr Fletcher, at his most ebullient, had presented the defenceless Laura and had had the nerve to say: 'Here's a little bride for Henry.'

Bride!

Laura had heard this story over and over again, and each time she had hated Hen Clarke more. She could scarcely forgive her father for projecting so dire a possibility and as a safeguard against it, she called Hen a drip and a nit whenever his name was mentioned. Mrs Fletcher defended him. 'Hen's no drip,' she said. 'He's a very nice boy, and clever. He's studying to be a research chemist and he'll go far. He'll be making big money when these smart alecs you admire are scraping along as salesmen and insurance agents.'

But Laura was not waiting for the bait of 'big money'; she would be off to London and out of Hen's reach long before he became a research chemist. In pledge of this, Laura borrowed Bouverie's *Guide To London* and going home, wrote in a notebook: 'London is not only another place, it's another planet', but on Thursday, London was forgotten again. With delight, and some surprise, Laura received a card from Vicky which said: 'How about the flicks on Saturday? If O.K., see you here 7 o'clock.'

On Saturday evening, when Laura appeared in her school uniform instead of her gilded polyvinyl chloride, Mrs Fletcher said: 'You're not going dancing tonight?'

'We thought we'd go to the pictures instead.'

'Sensible girls. But don't forget – never let me hear of you riding on that motor-bicycle.'

'What motor-bicycle?'

'You know very well what motor-bicycle.'

Laura did not reply. At Flamingo Park the housekeeper showed her into the living-room where Mr Logan was poring over his plan to extend the swimming-baths. He did not look up and Laura had to say: 'Good evening, Mr Logan.'

He raised his head and observed her through half moons of glass that made him seem aged and harassed. Moved to pity, she asked herself how could she ever reject him? She was not put to the test for he gave her a brief, conniving smile and returned his attention to his work.

Discouraged by the living, Laura went to Ronnie for comfort and Ronnie, obliging as ever, met her with a smile.

'Marry me, Laura,' said Ronnie's friendly gaze, 'and we'll go and live in London.' But there had been that sumptuous girl who smelled of gardenias. She, no doubt of it, would have seized on Ronnie long before Laura got the chance.

Feeling herself deprived of every man she met, Laura went into the hall and saw Vicky coming down the stairs in shirt and slacks.

'Where shall we go?' Vicky asked.

'The Odeon film looks good.'

'Oh, who wants to see a film on a night like this? We have all winter for cinemas.'

All winter for cinemas! With such a prospect, Laura would agree to anything: 'What do you suggest?'

'Let's go up on the downs.'

'We could have a walk.'

'Why not!'

At the roundabout outside Camperlea, Vicky veered left and Laura realized where they were going and why they were going there. From the rise of the bridge, she saw the great basin of the Creek, empty except for its rivulet of fresh water. The light, glossing the cushions of mud, the factory roof and the steel of the railway-lines, was richer in colour than it had been the first evening they came here. Already the season was changing. The summer, growing dusty, held no more surprises. In the past Laura had been saddened by the waning year but now it was all different. With Vicky for company, with the promise of a whole winter of cinemas, she need not care whether it was winter or summer.

Of course the autumn meant that Gilda would be back but Laura felt she could deal with Gilda now. Gilda had seen her as a stop-gap; Laura had treated her as a friend. If Gilda tried to thrust her out of the relationship, it would be a fight to a finish.

Once they had crossed the tracks, Vicky slowed down and they trundled towards the beat of the factory band. The usual hooting, skylarking group stood round the dance-hall steps, but one man stood alone. It was Clarrie, on the kerb, waiting as he had waited the week before. He was staring down the road towards them and as they drew near, he moved back a step, expecting them to stop; but Vicky did not stop. Instead, she put on speed and passed him without a glance. Laura looked back and saw his face crumple in baffled misery.

The lane swung them out of Clarrie's sight and Vicky came to a stop beneath a chestnut tree. Turning, she asked eagerly: 'Did you see him?'

'Yes.'

Vicky's cheeks were bright, her eyes brilliant. 'He was waiting for us, wasn't he?'

'He must have been.' Though she disliked him, Laura had been touched by Clarrie's pallid, watching face and said: 'Perhaps he wanted to apologize.'

'Do you think so?' Vicky was breathless with excitement: 'Shall we go back?'

151

'I don't think you should torment him.'

'Torment him! Do I torment him?' Vicky looked away: 'Better leave it. No point in starting all that up again.'

As they went on, following the rise towards the main road, Laura pondered Vicky's mention of 'all that', wondering how advanced, passionate and profound the brief liaison with Clarrie had been.

The country about them was chalky downland. On the other side of the main road the downs stretched all the way to Arundel. Laura and Valerie Whittam used to come up here on their bicycles to look for primroses or blackberries or any other prize that gave excuse for a walk. Crossing the main road more by luck than skill, Vicky took the short lane that ran up to the crest of the downs, stopping when the climb became too steep and leaving the machine in the hedge. Here the verges and hawthorn hedges were grey with chalk, the path rocky with noduled flints. At the top of the rise, where the path disappeared into the dusty grass, they could see miles of the folded downland on which Laura and Valerie had picked harebells and wild scabious.

With the evening before them, Laura thought she and Vicky might walk as far as the Roman chalk-pit that was supposed to be shaped like a finger pointing the way to Porchester; but Vicky had scarcely gone a dozen yards when she threw herself down on the grass and lay on her stomach, gazing back towards Salthouse.

This was the point on the road where people stopped to overlook the panorama of Camperlea. Mr Fletcher, when the Fletchers came here for picnics, liked to point out the six church spires and the concrete cupolas of the town hall.

This evening the Creek showed as a map of mud, a useless moat separating the new town of Salthouse with its white-silver factory-tops from Camperlea where the roofs ran like furrows between the gas-works and the shore. The scene seemed washed with chalk so everything was of a colour. Even the sea, which fingered in all along the coast, was the same flat azure as the scabious and hare-bells.

'There *are* better views,' said Vicky.

'I suppose there are.' Laura, who had not seen them, thought the long, pasty-pale expanse of coast quite im-pressive. The Island, a shadow on the other side of the Solent, set her thinking of Mrs Toplady who might at that moment be wearing her crimson dress and smoking a cigar and looking out to sea.

Vicky rolled on to her back and yawned: 'What shall we do now?'

'What do you want to do?'

'Well!' Vicky appeared to be considering the question but Laura knew what the answer would be. 'Shall we . . .' Vicky picked a grass blade and chewed it: 'Shall we go and look in to the hall? We won't dance or anything. We'll just see if he's there.'

'You know he's there.'

'I'd like to see what he does when he sees us.'

'He'll be beastly, as always. I don't want to go. Really, Vicky, I'd rather go for a walk.'

'But I thought you enjoyed the dance. You said you had fun there.'

'I did, in a way; but the men are strange. They're grotty. They don't want to talk. You can't get anything out of them.'

'They don't go there to talk.

'But one wants to talk some time. I mean, you want to learn about people. You want to discover things. I'd like to know where they come from, what sort of homes they have. I want to hear their ideas. I'd like to know what they're thinking.'

'Grief! No wonder they say you're crazy.'

'They say I'm crazy!'

Laura was so dismayed that Vicky redeemed her remark: 'One of them said you were a crazy chick.'

'Oh, that's different. That's another sort of crazy. It doesn't mean I'm a . . . a steaming nit.'

Vicky laughed: 'Anyway, they like you. One of them said you were cute.'

'Cute!' Laura was disgusted. She was not one to be patronized; she intended to excel.

'Well?' Vicky returned to her desired topic: 'Shall we go down and see how Clarrie behaves?'

Uneasy at the thought of a return to Clarrie Piper, Laura found courage to protest: 'I don't know what you see in him. He's not even a dish. Lots of the other fellows are better looking.'

Vicky said, 'That's true,' but she smiled to herself as though everything Laura said served only to increase Clarrie's attraction for her. 'Still, there's something about him – I don't know what. I keep feeling that if I see him again, I'll know what it is.'

'I wonder what Gilda would think of him?'

Vicky seemed delighted by the thought of Gilda pronouncing on Clarrie. 'She'd hate him.' Springing to her feet, she put out a hand to pull Laura up: 'Come on.'

'We're not properly dressed.'

'Who cares!' Vicky, for all her indolence, was a girl who got her own way.

As they coasted down into Salthouse, the sun was setting. The lights came on in the hall. The windows, golden with light, were all open and the noise of the band struck the girls as they left the B.S.A. in the parking lot. Vicky, brilliant with anticipation, said to Laura: 'You didn't really want to walk over those draggy old downs, did you?'

'I suppose not.'

Vicky hurried into the hall, impatient now to see Clarrie, but Clarrie was not to be seen. The interior air was stifling. The floor was crowded with people lying or sitting, too dulled by the heat to do more. The dancers formed pockets of activity among the crowd but even they would gesture for a while then drift into inactivity. Vicky, pushing among them, looking this way and that, seemed gay and amused, but when she realized Clarrie was not there, weariness came down on her. She glanced behind and finding Laura at her heels, said: 'Come on. Let's go.' They were starting back when one of the men seized on her saying, 'Give, baby,' and the music crashed out again.

Laura sat on the floor with the others and watched Vicky who responded to her partner but looked as though her movements were slowed by the heavy atmosphere. A shadow lay over her and her smile was meaningless. A whisper came to Laura under the noise of the band: 'There's Piper.' She looked round, guessing that someone had gone to tell him Vicky was here. He was in the doorway, surveying the hall with black, suspicious looks.

Laura reached out and touched Vicky who turned at once. Laura pointed to Clarrie. Without a word to her partner, her face revivified, Vicky sped among the seated figures and Clarrie, catching sight of her, turned his face from her and started to undulate to the music. Keeping his elbows in to his waist, he worked his forearms like pistons and moved his shoulders and hips with fluid sensuality,

155

all the time rubbing the thumb of each hand upon its neighbouring finger-tip. He seemed aware of nothing but the pulsing uproar from the group on the stage.

Placing herself before him and bending down so she could smile up into his face, Vicky began to imitate his movements but as she began, he stopped abruptly, turned and walked out of the hall. She stood still, her face piteous, then started to follow him but Laura caught her up before she reached the door and said: 'Don't go.'

'I must speak to him. I must explain.'

Fearful of what might happen if Vicky left the protecting crowd, Laura held to her and she let herself be led to where her partner awaited her. She raised her hands, doing her best to seem carefree, and danced again but at the next pause in the music, she hurried to Laura and said: 'It's getting late.'

By now, Laura thought, Clarrie would have taken himself off but as they left the hall, they met him coming back into it. He blocked the doorway and watching Vicky's approach with a cold, speculative stare, said: 'Going some place?'

Vicky kept her head down so her face was hidden by her hair. She said: 'We're going home.'

'In a hurry, aren't we?'

'No. It's nearly ten. Laura has to be back, you know.'

'You got plentyer time. You want to dance, so come on. Dance.'

'No. We're going.'

He would not move to let her past. As she made to edge round him, he caught her arm and pulled her back into the dance. The music started. He began to work his body and forearms, rubbing thumb and finger as before, while she stood motionless, watching as though she had no part in it.

156

He caught her by the wrist and jerked her towards him but she merely smiled, waiting to be allowed to go. Some of the dancers paused and looked at them with furtive curiosity then when Clarrie stared round in annoyance, they laughed outright. Challenged, he put his hands on Vicky's shoulders and shook her as though trying to shake her into some sort of rhythm, but she hung limp under his hands, smiling her mild smile, infuriating him until suddenly, with a swift and violent lunge, he wrapped his arms round her and kissed her on the mouth. It was a furious embrace, expressing anger not love, and for the first time she was stirred to action. She struggled and pushed at him with her hands but she could not get free.

One of the men leant close to Clarrie's ear and gave a wolf whistle that cut piercingly through the music and Clarrie swung round, releasing Vicky who fell back, pale, unsmiling, and wiped her mouth with her handkerchief.

The men around were shocked, not by Clarrie's truculence but by Vicky and her automatic reaction to the embrace.

Clarrie, finding no enemy ready for him, turned on Vicky again and seizing hold of her and looking down into her face, seemed about to spit. Her smile returned and this time, beside himself, he caught her hair, gripping a handful of it near the roots, and with the other hand started to strike her face. He struck her again and again. Though flung about so her neck seemed to be broken, she still smiled, letting herself be beaten to one side and the other, making no move to defend herself.

Laura could see in Clarrie the same virulent rancour that he had brought to his attack on the hangar. Infected by his violence, she rushed at him, fists raised, but one of the men pushed her aside and catching Clarrie by the scruff, pulled

157

him back as though he were a scrimmaging dog. He swung round again and the men closed in on him. As Vicky fell free, Laura caught her arm and hurried her from the hall. They went unnoticed.

In the dark open air, Vicky paused and shook her head, trying to regain her senses. She was too dazed to speak and Laura, respecting the heroine of such a drama, kept silent. Inside the hall the music faltered and came to a stop. Hearing a tumult of blows and shouts, Laura whispered, 'For goodness sake, Vicky, let's get away from here,' and they ran to the parking lot.

At the end of Rowantree Avenue, Laura asked: 'Did he hurt you much?'

Vicky gave an exhausted guff of laughter: 'I don't know.'

'He's mad. Absolutely bonkers. I wish you'd stop seeing him, Vicky. Surely you don't *have* to see him?'

'No.'

'One thing to be thankful for – he doesn't know where you live. If we don't go back to Salthouse, he can't find you.'

'I suppose not. Let's talk about it another time. Come to tea on Wednesday?'

Not wanting to be seen by her mother until her excitement had died down, Laura loitered under the rowan trees and thought bitterly about Clarrie Piper. He had despoiled and destroyed the summer, the summer when, by a miracle, Vicky had been left in her care. Had there been no Clarrie to steal Vicky's interest and browbeat and ill-treat her, what happiness she and Vicky might have shared!

'The vicar!' she muttered. 'The grotty old vicar with his grotty good works!' But she had to admit that though the vicar had brought Clarrie to the St Barnabas' dance, it was she, Laura, who had brought Clarrie to Vicky's notice.

The miraculous chance and the evil mischance had cancelled each other out.

The best she could wish was never to see Clarrie Piper again, but she did see him and very much sooner than she would have thought possible. It was on Monday, in the grey and steamy evening, while the washing tossed and turned in the washing-machine, Laura, wandering out to Doris Road, imagining a chance encounter with someone who looked like Mr Logan, came instead upon Clarrie walking the back streets of North Camperlea. He was coming towards her, leaning slightly forward as though seeking something that might be only a short distance away. He was so absorbed in his search that his glance passed over her without recognizing her. He knew only that she was not what he was looking for. She stepped into a shop doorway and watched him go past, then followed him. He paused first at the corner of Elizabeth Street, then at Marion Road and again at Lucille Place, each time staring down the length of dismal house rows like a mariner that looks to the horizon. Finding nothing that he wanted to find, he went towards Berwick Road. Laura, stalking him with the zest of a hunter, saw him stop at Berwick Road and turn his long, searching gaze first right, then left. To the left something caught his attention. He hastened out of sight. Running to the corner, Laura saw him examining a B.S.A. motor-bicycle that was propped against one of the little half-bay houses. He stood for some minutes, very still, his eyes fixed on the machine but it was dirty and almost derelict; he knew it was not the right one.

When he had asked where she lived, Vicky had waved in this direction, but could he really imagine she lived here, among these chalk scribbled walls and shabby scraps of 'garden'? It occurred to Laura that he may have grown up in an area so wretched that even the North Camperlea back streets looked prosperous to him and a likely home for Vicky.

She did not follow him any farther. Gazing after him as he went searching on, she thought how strange he looked away from Salthouse, and he seemed conscious of his own strangeness. His walk, a swaggering lope, menacing yet cautious, might be fashionable where he came from, but in Berwick Road, among the self-respecting conventional poor, he looked like a jungle creature that had slipped its cage but found freedom more bewildering than captivity.

How many evenings had he wasted in this hopeless search for Vicky? Laura, seeing him out of sight, could only pity him.

Now she had reason to telephone Vicky. She started to run to the call-box then stopped in her tracks. Vicky would pity him as Laura did, and pity would take her back to Salthouse.

Had Wednesday been a fine day, a day for lying and talking on the lawn, Laura would have been tempted to tell Vicky about her sight of Clarrie, but Wednesday did not encourage confidences. The summer's complacency had been shaken by a storm and a high wind was blustering about the front. Mrs Logan and her women friends were playing bridge in the living-room, Vicky was given a ten-shilling note and the girls were told to get their tea at the Clematis.

They strolled through Flamingo Park where an old naval man was launching his model battleship upon the lake. Vicky, who seemed uneasy and distracted, paused to watch as the ship zigzagged cleverly among the children's boats, leaving behind a smell of methylated spirits. She smiled from habit but her attention was not really on the little ship, or on Laura, or on anything in sight. She did not try to talk and Laura, feeling herself an unwanted guest, could think of nothing to say until they reached the arcade, the notorious arcade in which Mr Fletcher's thousand had sunk without trace. It was still called the amusement arcade but amusements were few in Camperlea. Looking inside, Laura saw the summer visitors sitting in deck-chairs, packed together, sheltering from the vexatious wind and staring out at the grey, tumultuous sea.

'What a town!' she sighed, wondering if there were any other place on earth where two girls, one as lovely as Vicky, both young and eager for life, could find nothing to do but walk an eventless strip of concrete and take tea at the draggy old Clematis. 'Vicky,' she begged, 'you must come to London. You must, you must, you must!'

'The wind blows in London, too.'

'Yes, but it doesn't matter there. Think of all the art galleries and museums and coffee bars and cinemas and theatres and dance clubs and fabulous men! Honestly, Vicky, if . . .' She wanted to say 'If you lived in London, you wouldn't waste a glance on Clarrie Piper' but she thought better of it and lamely added: 'You will come, won't you?'

'It's not very likely.'

'But you can't stay here. You're wasted in a place like this. The people here are so dim they don't even know how beautiful you are. But even if they did, what difference would it make? There's nothing for you here.'

All places are much the same. Wherever you are, you're just living.'

Laura cried out, appalled by such lack of enterprise. Could Vicky not feel the wonder of her own beauty? Or know the opportunities that beauty could give? She was like some exquisite animal that had no knowledge of its own perfection: a Saluki or a Siamese cat or an African leopard, flawless in shape yet concerned only with its digestive system and its reproductive system and the exercise of its muscles.

'Grief! Don't you want to be famous?'

Vicky smiled: 'What on earth could I be famous for?'

'For your looks, of course. You could be a film star or a model girl. You could marry a millionaire if you wanted to. You want to get married, don't you? Well, there's no one worth marrying in Camperlea.'

Vicky glanced past Laura and fixed her smile on the dismal sea. Her eyes, very dark in this light, narrowed as though viewing something a long way away, something Laura could not see. Her expression, amused and knowing, was so strange that Laura wondered if she knew Vicky at all. Were they really friends? Was the friendship anything more than a fantasy of Laura's own? After a long silence, Vicky said: 'I might marry Clarrie Piper.'

'You're joking.'

'I don't know. The funny thing is: I *could* marry him.'

'What would your parents think?'

'What indeed?' Vicky laughed. The idea of this marriage, now that it was in her mind, seemed to act like an intoxicant. She looked so brilliant and gay that Laura felt a sense of outrage.

'And you'd live in Salthouse among those grotty women?'

'Not necessarily. Clarrie makes a lot of money. Some weeks, with overtime, he gets forty or fifty quid.'

'I don't believe it.'

'It's true. He showed me a pay slip.'

Laura brooded on the fact that Clarrie had for his own use more money than a man like her father, with wife and children to support. The money gave Clarrie an intolerable advantage. Laura could see the marriage was possible – just possible – and she protested against it: 'You could marry anyone. Don't you realize that? Someone as beautiful as you could do anything.'

'Oh, beautiful! There's nothing in being beautiful. People stare at you but what good does that do? What difference does it make?'

'I suppose you only know that if you're not beautiful.'

Vicky spoke seriously: 'You know, Laura, you think looks are more important than they really are. However beautiful you are, you're still a human being.'

'Eating, sleeping and digesting?'

'Exactly. If I marry, I might as well marry someone who makes me feel something.'

'And Clarrie makes you feel something?'

'Yes.'

'Oh, Vicky! You make *me* feel miserable.'

'I'm sorry. I know you don't like him. I don't even like him myself. I don't want him to touch me – and yet I want to see him again.'

'So you want to go back to Salthouse?'

'Just once more. But don't leave me alone with him.'

Laura sighed and was silent. She remembered that Vicky had lent her a handkerchief and after a moment solemnly said: 'Vicky, you know I will do anything you want.'

'Then let's go on Saturday. Let me take one more look at him. Let me get him out of my system.'

'All right.'

It seemed to Laura that next Saturday would be one more Saturday wasted. In no time Gilda would be home and Laura would no longer be Vicky's Best Friend. Yet, thinking of Gilda, it occurred to her that Gilda might be the answer to this business. She would not tolerate Clarrie as rival. And there was a chance she would want him for herself. She had been interested in him when she saw him and, with her noisy vitality and coarse good looks, she might be the very girl for Clarrie. She would not madden him with a tolerant lack of response; and she was physically strong. If Clarrie hit her, she would probably hit him back with a will. Laura's spirits rose as she thought of Gilda dealing with Clarrie. Suddenly the Clematis, with its chintz and old oak and smell of toasted tea-cake, seemed a delightful place and she felt she could safely tell about seeing Clarrie in the back streets of North Camperlea.

'What was he doing?' Vicky asked.

'Just prowling around. There was an old B.S.A. and when he saw it wasn't your bike, he was pretty glum.'

'You don't think he was looking for me?'

'Who else?' Laura spoke lightly then regretted she had spoken at all. Vicky ceased to smile. She looked like someone caught by the closing of a trap.

Laura's golden dress had lost so much gold, it appeared to be smudged with black. At the sight of it on Saturday evening, Mrs Fletcher said: 'So you're off to that St

Barnabas' Dance again! I thought you'd stopped that nonsense. You've got to work, you know. You'll have to start thinking of your A levels.'

'Grief,' Laura said, 'I've only just taken my O levels.'

That morning notice had come that Laura had been awarded six O levels and Mrs Fletcher, surprised by this result, said in satisfaction: 'There's no knowing what anyone can do till they try.' Her ambitions, so long fixed on Tom, veered upon Laura whose sole purpose at that moment was to get to Flamingo Park.

'You're the one who wants to change the world,' said Mrs Fletcher; 'now's your chance. If you put your mind to it, you might get to a university.'

Laura came to a stop. Even Flamingo Park was forgotten. 'You'd never let me go.'

'Why do you say that?'

'You never let me do anything. You're always saying I've got to hurry up and earn my living. If I went to a university, I wouldn't be earning. In fact, you'd have to help me.'

'You'd get a grant.'

'Yes, but those grants aren't enough.'

'We'll see,' Mrs Fletcher was cheerful and promising. 'When the time comes, we'll see.'

This was a possibility beyond anything. Laura felt dazed as she walked down Rowantree Avenue and when she saw the bus pass at the end, made no effort to catch it. There would be another.

Her first reaction to her mother's project was almost disappointment because the future could be made too easy. She had prepared herself for struggle and now it seemed she would not have to struggle, but as her uncertainty passed, she began to feel an amazed joy at the chance that might be offered her. There had been reports in the *Herald* of students of the Camperlea Technical College who had gone to a university in Sussex. And Sussex was no distance at all. If she went there, she would still be near enough to Flamingo Park. She began to see how she could retain friendship yet fulfil ambition. She would have to work, of course, but she was willing to work. She became tranquil with the sense that her mother had given her something – or was willing to give her something. It was as though hostilities were resolving themselves at last.

Mrs Logan, her alcove aglow with early evening, said: 'Why, Laura, how are you, dear?'

Laura opened her mouth and was about to tell Mrs Logan about the O levels and the university when Vicky came into the room. She looked pale but it was a velvet pallor, enhanced by the green fire of earrings and sequins and Mrs Logan, turning to look at her, gave a gasp of pleasure. Vicky tried to block her mother's admiration by saying to Laura 'You look nice,' but Mrs Logan insisted on being heard:

'How wonderful to be a girl again!' Her glance passing in a kindly way over Laura and coming to rest on her own child, she said: 'Young, beautiful and innocent; above all, innocent. It is only as you get older that you learn how cruel life can be.'

'Poor pettikins!' Vicky put her hands down on her mother's hands and, bending, kissed her on the cheek. 'You have had more than your share, haven't you, pet? But all over now.'

Her mother held to her: 'I hope . . . I do hope when you girls marry, you'll know what it is to have daughters of your own.' She looked at Laura and blinked moisture

166

from her eyes: 'Without Vicky, I'd never have pulled through.'

When they were out of Mrs Logan's hearing, Laura said: 'I do love your mother.'

'Yes, she's an old sweetiekins,' Vicky agreed, but casually, her mind on other things. There was about her a self-conscious tension as though she were facing an ex-cruciating but desired ordeal. In her haste to meet it, she drove at a pace unusual for her and reduced her speed only when she saw Clarrie was waiting, as usual, on the kerb. He was looking down the road and as the motor-cycle drew near, he made no move. His face was expressionless; he seemed prepared for Vicky to drive past. When she stopped, he let out his breath and curtly said: 'I want a word with you.'

'All right,' Vicky nodded, 'but I have to take the bike inside.'

'No, I'll deal with it. And you,' he indicated Laura. 'This don't concern you. You clear off.'

Vicky muttered, 'Don't go,' and Laura, getting down from the pillion, moved a little way off but did not enter the hall. Clarrie, thinking she was disposed of, said: 'I was dead choked last week. I was mad.'

It was an apology of sorts. Vicky smiled and Clarrie was about to speak again when he noticed that Laura was still with them. Frowning, he flicked a commanding finger at her: 'Didn't I tell you to clear off? Go on in. Give the boys a treat. She'll join you later.'

Laura looked directly at Vicky: 'What do you want me to do?'

'Wait there. We won't be long.'

'Why you want that kid around, I don't know.' Clarrie propped the B.S.A. against the kerb and taking Vicky by the elbow, led her across to the opposite pavement. They stopped outside the factory gate and Laura sat down on the hut steps to keep watch. She was in shadow; they in sunlight. It was like watching a dumb charade.

Vicky, with her back against the high, steel-meshed fence of the factory, listened with head bent so her curtains of hair fell forward and masked her face; Clarrie, in front of her, talked earnestly. People passing glanced at them with curiosity, and some even stopped to stare at Vicky and Vicky's shimmering hair. Every time there was a pause in the footsteps, Clarrie looked round until, exasperated, he began to urge Vicky to go somewhere where they would not be seen. She shook her head and remained as she was, her backside propped against the fence, her legs stretched taut in front of her.

Several times Laura saw Vicky shake her head and as her hair swayed, the light seemed to glance about her and about her silk frock and her long legs now brown with summer. Clarrie, it seemed, was losing patience, but as he stood over her in an attitude of graceless irritation, Vicky looked up, threw back her hair, and laughed in his face.

Laura decided that she need not fear for Vicky. For all his bullying, Vicky could do what she liked with Clarrie.

Bert, coming up the steps in his red corduroy jeans, said: 'Hello, what you doing out here?'

'I'm waiting for Vicky.'

'Late, is she?'

'No, she's over there with Clarrie Piper.'

Glancing across the road, Bert grinned: 'Don't waste your time, kid. Come on in.'

Laura could feel the drum-beat vibrating through the

wooden porch. Now that she had a chance to go accompanied, she was drawn to the dance, but she said: 'I must wait for Vicky. She's my friend.'

'You're a funny one.'

Laura excused herself: 'She said she wouldn't be long.'

'Don't bet on it. If I know Piper, she won't be back before tomorrow morning. Come on. Give it up.'

Laura shook her head and Bert gave Vicky another glance: 'She's worth waiting for all right. If I were you, I'd tell her to watch out.'

'She won't listen to me.'

Bert shrugged and, grinning, went inside.

Now a group of men paused to chat by the factory gates and Clarrie, affronted by their nearness, shouted something and turned away. He crossed the road towards the B.S.A. and Vicky ran after him. Straddling the machine, standing with the saddle between his thighs, he jerked his head at the pillion and said: 'Get on.'

Seeing Vicky obey, Laura jumped to her feet, shouting: 'Take me with you.'

'Nope. I told you: go on in. Give the boys a treat.' He repeated this jeer with an irony that was the only humour known to him.

Ignoring him, Laura said: 'Don't go without me, Vicky. Bert said you ought to watch out.'

Vicky murmured, 'Yes,' and after a moment, added: 'I want Laura to come with us.'

Clarrie drew in an angry breath then looked across at the men outside the factory gates. He seemed to be considering the situation, his cheek muscles working with the effort of thought, then his expression cleared. Reaching a decision, he smiled to himself.

'Right.' He gave Laura a derisive look and said: 'Get

on the tank then; and keep your head down if you don't want to lose it.'

It was obvious when he started off that this time he knew exactly where he was going. He turned into Salthouse lane, taking the turn at an angle that nearly threw Laura off her perch. She held on obstinately, feeling his desire to be rid of her, and knowing if she fell, he would not stop to retrieve her. They passed the allotments and the brickfield, then Clarrie slowed and looked about him. When they came to the cottages, he stopped and pushing at Laura's shoulder, said: 'This is where you get off.'

'Why?'

'We want to talk private, see? You wait here.'

'I don't want to wait here.'

'You don't want to do nothing, do you?' Clarrie's irony was venomous. He gave Laura another push to hasten her descent but she gripped the tank with her knees, tightened her hold on the handle-bars, and said:

'I'm not leaving Vicky.'

Clarrie put his hands to her waist and lifted her up from the tank as he might lift a cup from a hook. Afraid if he dropped her, she would fall face to the ground, she was forced to lift one foot over the tank. In a moment she was standing in the road.

She turned and appealed to Vicky who had watched her swift displacement with bewildered eyes. 'Vicky, you told me to stay with you. Do you want me to wait here?'

'We can't leave her here alone.' Vicky made a move to get off the pillion but she was too slow. Clarrie shot away and she had to cling to him to save herself from falling.

Looking back, Clarrie shouted: 'We won't be long.' Now that he had got what he wanted, he sounded hilarious and, reassured by his tone, Laura watched the machine swerve round the bend and out of sight; then listened to the throb of the engine as it faded in the distance. She supposed they would stop at the Creek and lean over the Creek wall and talk intimately together. If they were not to be long, she did not mind waiting here. Freed from the hateful, overhanging nearness of Clarrie, she could even enjoy solitude.

The lowering sunlight fell richly over the dead orchard. The brick of the orchard wall had a garnet glow. It was always just here, at this point, with the Creek still a mile away, that the sky seemed to open up and became higher and wider than other skies. Even in cloudy weather, Laura had felt that the light over the undulating orchard increased the spaciousness of space. But this evening the illusion could not last much longer. Already the sky was growing yellow; damp was rising and the close, misty air seemed to shut out sound.

Now there was nothing to be heard, Laura went to the cottages and looked for diversion. A few yards behind them there were the remains of a walled-in kitchen garden where Tom and she, climbing about among the crumbling brickwork, had found gooseberries and currants growing in a tangle of undergrowth. There might be some now but she feared, if she were out of sight, Vicky and Clarrie would go on, thinking she had walked back to Salthouse.

The last occupants of the cottages had padlocked the doors and shuttered the windows; all to no purpose. They had been empty so long, the roofs had fallen in. Now the front door had been broken open, the shutters had dropped on their hinges and the rooms were open to intruders. Laura, looking in through a window frame, saw nothing but dust and shadow. At the side of one cottage there was a fig tree covered with small green bottle shapes. Dozens more had fallen to the ground. She gathered a handful and amused herself by biting them open and finding the miniature seeds inside. She tried with her tongue to recognize some recondite fig flavour but they were not even bitter. They tasted of nothing and she threw them one by one into an upper window.

A smell of autumn had come into the air and the twilight was gathering. She began to grow tired of solitude and sat down on the grass verge, feeling she had waited long enough. The silence was oppressive. The sensible thing, she knew, would be to start walking back while there was still light. Probably the others would catch up on her. She thought about it but could not leave the spot where Vicky had left her. She had to be found waiting exactly where Vicky expected to find her. It was not just a question of loyalty. She wanted Clarrie to know that Vicky had a vigilant friend.

When the ground felt chilly beneath her, she rose and walked to the bend in the road round which the motorcycle had passed from view. Dusk had fallen but a ghostly light still hung over the orchard grass and the trees looked incandescent. She could see the roof of the distant hangar. She thought of walking on in the hope of meeting Vicky and Clarrie, but if she did not meet them, she would have that much farther to walk back. She returned to the cottages, knowing it was now so late, even if she set out to walk the night would overtake her long before she reached Salthouse. She began to think of Mrs Fletcher's hints and warnings about 'bad men'. She trembled, feeling cold, and listened and longed for Vicky to come, and remembered fearful stories about haunted roads.

When it was almost dark she heard a motor-bicycle in the remote distance and her nerves leapt in relief. They were coming at last. But the sound trickled away from her and when it was lost in the distance, she saw a light raying and moving upwards where the lane joined the main road. She watched it until it disappeared.

That could only be Vicky's B.S.A. for no other traffic had come along the lane. They must have decided to return by the main road. She could not bear to think they had forgotten her. She told herself they just could not imagine she would wait here all the time. They thought she had walked back to Salthouse. Anyway, here she was, abandoned, alone.

Surely, when they found she was not in the dance hall, they would return for her, all the more surprised at her tenacity.

But it was too late for fantasies now. Something rustled in the grass. People said that after dark the rats ran in packs over the old allotments. At the thought of walking back past the brickfields and the chalk-pits and the rat-infested fields, fear rose in her like a sickness.

Still, she had to get home. She did not know the time but she had a sinking sense that hours had passed since they left her there. Hours and hours. At the thought of her mother's anxiety, the rats appeared innocuous. She started back to Salthouse at a run.

The moon, edging up from the horizon like a coin pressing into a slot, gave enough light to mark the path but it was indefinite light. Several times she found herself lost in the long grass with the rats and spiders.

The moon, a gibbous moon, horribly blacked out on one side, rose quickly and lightened the brickfield and the brickfield chimney, a threatening phallus, and the distant greyish clay hills.

Stumbling on the grass roots and invisible road ruts,

she sobbed: 'Vicky, Vicky, Vicky.' Yet she was sure there must be some explanation of Vicky's conduct and to-morrow, hearing what had happened, her distress would dissolve as nightmare dissolves on waking.

Hearing a lorry pass on the Salthouse road, she wiped her eyes in relief. She could see the greenish-blue glow of the street lights. When she reached the end of the lane, she felt she was leaving a region of infernal dangers. She could scarcely believe she had survived it.

Salthouse was asleep. The dance hall was shut. That meant it was past midnight. Of course Vicky would have thought she had gone home.

There was no sign of life at the station. No hope of a bus. Laura walked at a furious pace and reached the bridge. That was one point passed, one obstacle overcome. After the bridge came the long road to the roundabout. Here, in the purlieus of the gas-works, were all the dismal offices that Camperlea kept out of sight: the lunatic asylum, the old workhouse and the Fever Hospital that was empty because no one had fever nowadays. These fearful buildings could only be seen from the top of the bus and the Fletcher children used to look out on them with awe. They had been shut away from pedestrian gaze by a high regular wall that seemed to Laura never ending. It did end and then there came the railings of Camperlea cemetery, slabs and crosses glimmering inside. Opposite was the gasometer and all the paraphernalia of the gas-works. The roundabout brought her into the dull, half-rural road that eventually became the High Street. The first shops filled her with gratitude. All else was home. Now there remained to be overcome only the half-mile walk down Rowantree Avenue.

The best she could hope for was that her parents had

gone to bed. Even if in bed, Mrs Fletcher would be awake and listening, ready to call accusingly, 'Where have you been, I'd like to know?' but Laura thought if she mumbled something like: 'Tell you tomorrow', she might get to her own room and leave explanations to the morning. There was no light on the upper floor. No light anywhere. Foolishly she began to hope that everyone was asleep. She had her key ready and tried to turn it in the lock without making a sound; but even as the door opened, all hope was destroyed. A crack of light showed under the living-room door. She could have run upstairs but flight would only make matters worse. She must enter the sitting-room and face the scene within.

Mrs Fletcher was standing by the fireplace, one elbow on the shelf, her face buried in her hands. Tom, in his pyjamas, stood beside her, a protective arm round her waist. He looked up reproachfully as Laura appeared but there was a hint of mischief in his look. She was for it. If Tom had been got out of bed, things were bad indeed.

Mrs Fletcher slowly raised her head to show a flushed wet face and fixed Laura with terrible eyes.

'You wicked girl.'

Laura dared not speak. And she was too tired to speak; but even if she were not too tired, what could she say?

Having made her indictment, Mrs Fletcher sank down into a chair. She had exhausted herself and suddenly she wept, helplessly, her shoulders shaking, her head in her hands. Tom began to cry in sympathy.

Laura watched, aghast. She could not discount her mother's emotion; it was real. This was something Laura had refused to believe. She had always told herself that her mother's anxiety was forced, that she did not really care whether Laura was here or not. Now Laura had to admit that in spite of the drama and the heightened anxiety, her mother had suffered. It would have mattered to her had Laura had an accident, or run away to London.

Near collapse, Laura slid down to the opposite chair and sat in desolate apathy, discomfited at being more indebted than she knew. Although her attention was on her mother and Tom, she felt something missing in the room. Her father ought to be there. His absence seemed to her so sinister, she found voice to ask: 'Where's Daddy?'

'Ah!' Mrs Fletcher sat up and wiped her eyes. 'You may well ask "Where's Daddy?"'

Laura became faint with the fear that he was dead. And she, of course, was to blame. Terrified that somehow, by some means, her late return had brought about his death, she begged 'Where is he?' and her breaking voice caused Mrs Fletcher to relent.

'I sent him down to St Barnabas' Church. I told him to go to the vicarage and let them know what we think about them keeping you there to this hour. And I told him to find where those Logans live and go and give them a piece of his mind. . . .' Mrs Fletcher paused, breathless with self-justification, and Laura broke in:

'*How could you?* Mummy, how could you? The buses have stopped. He'll have to walk all the way there and back . . .'

'How dare you speak to me like that?' Beside herself at hearing the accused turn accuser, Mrs Fletcher now let her rage run free: 'Why did he have to go? Whose fault was it? Where have you been, I'd like to know? It's nearly one o'clock. One o'clock! Just think of it! A girl of your age roaming the streets at this hour! What have you been up to?'

'I haven't been up to anything. I was out with Vicky. We missed the last bus. I had to walk.'

'Ah!' Mrs Fletcher was still enraged but her tone was changing. At the possibility of an innocent explanation of Laura's conduct, she became calm enough to think of Tom and said to him: 'Go to bed now, darling. You've been a great comfort to your mother.'

Tom, thinking the excitement was at an end, kissed her and went without argument. As soon as he was gone, Mrs Fletcher demanded explanation:

'You missed the last bus, you say. The last bus goes at eleven-thirty. You should have been home long before that. What were you doing down there all that time?'

Laura considered possible excuses: the dance-hall clock wrong, the dance-hall on fire, Mrs Logan taken ill and Vicky and Laura called to her aid! Each could be disproved later and lead to more trouble. She said: 'We didn't go to the dance. We went for a walk. We went to Salthouse.'

'Salthouse! That place where the factory people come from?'

'Yes. Vicky has a friend there. He said he wanted to talk to her and she asked me to go with her. They went away to talk and they didn't come back. I didn't know what to do. I didn't know the time. When I went to the bus stop, the last bus had gone. I had to walk all the way.'

'A nice thing!' Mrs Fletcher showed some triumph in the fact that her worst fears had not been groundless but Laura was not the culprit. 'A nice thing indeed! That Vicky Logan goes off with a fellow and leaves you to walk home alone! I hope you see no more of that one.'

'I'm sure there was a reason.'

'Oh, I'm sure there was. No doubt of it. There was a

reason, all right.' Her voice rising in derisive contempt, Mrs Fletcher was all set to expose Vicky Logan when the front door opened. She stopped to listen and said with satisfaction: 'There's your father now. He wasn't so long, after all.'

Then they became aware that Mr Fletcher was not alone. Mrs Fletcher dried her face, straightened her dress and cardigan and composed herself for the reception of a visitor.

The living-room door opened. At the sight of Laura, her father sighed in relief: 'So you're all right, Lory, but where's your friend?'

'Isn't Vicky home yet?'

Mr Logan was behind him; a changed Mr Logan, grey-faced and severe. Now there was no conniving smile for Laura. Laura was safely home, Vicky was not; and he looked at Laura like an accusing counsel: 'Where did you leave my daughter?' he sternly asked.

Mrs Fletcher flew to Laura's defence: 'It was your daughter who left my Laura. She went off with some fellow and my daughter had to walk home alone.'

Mr Fletcher lifted his hand in appeal: 'We must have the whole story. There's a police car outside. The police will want to know what's happened. Now, Lory, out with it.'

Laura told the exact truth and Mrs Fletcher, learning how she had been deceived, spoke once only: 'So you went on that motor-cycle after all I said.' Mr Fletcher lifted his hand again and she was silenced.

Laura, who had described the light of the motor-bicycle going up to the main road, said: 'They may have eloped. They may have gone to Brighton.'

Mr Logan ignored these possibilities. He asked: 'Where is this lane you went to?'

178

'It's Salthouse Lane. Tom and I used to go there before the factory was built. You remember it, Daddy?' Laura turned to her father who was looking very tired. A tear had flowed from his injured eye and he wiped his cheek. 'You used to take us there.'

'Well, yes. I think I know where you mean.' He seemed to have lost his memory of the lane but, as ever, willing to oblige, he said: 'I expect I can find it . . .'

Abrupt with apprehensions, Mr Logan broke in: 'We can't waste time looking about. She knows where it is. *She* saw where Vicky went. She'll have to come with us.'

Dismayed at the thought of returning to the darkness of the lane, Laura protested: 'But Vicky can't be there now. If she didn't go with Clarrie, she would have come to the cottages. She knew I was waiting for her.' When her father did not speak, Laura looked to her mother but Mrs Fletcher was in no mood to protect her.

'You must show them where you went. It's your duty to help the police.' Another time she might have taken pity on Laura but now she felt that the girl must be made to realize how serious it was to deceive a mother.

No one spoke inside the car as it covered with easy speed the road which Laura had walked so painfully. The sergeant and his driver sat in front. Laura, packed into the back between Mr Logan and her father, was as close to Vicky's father as she could hope to be; but it meant nothing. He sat forward, a taut, withdrawn and gloomy figure that bore no relation to the fascinating Mr Logan who had swept her off her feet.

The police were not local men. They had said they knew

the factory but they did not know the Salthouse lane. On the other side of the railway tracks, the sergeant asked where they should go now.

Laura said: 'The lane's past the factory. It runs down to the Creek.'

'And this man Piper! Where does he live?'

Laura did not know and Mr Logan moved irritably, protesting against the delay: 'If we want to find Piper, we can find him later. What we want now is to find my daughter.'

'All in good time,' said the sergeant. 'Suppose the young lady's gone to his lodgings. We'd look a right bunch of nits trailing up this lane and her tucked up warm – in a manner of speaking, that is, of course.'

Mr Logan said no more as they drove to the local police station, discovered the whereabouts of the factory foreman and from him found Clarrie Piper's address.

The moon was well up now. Waning and crooked, it cast not so much light as a ghastly gloom over the raw council estate. Clarrie's landlady threw up a first-floor window and looked out in querulous inquiry but when she saw the police at the door, she became conciliatory and shouted: 'I'll be down at once' then, turning from the window, she said to someone inside: 'It's that Piper again. They've got a girl in the car.'

Laura, the girl in the car, felt the importance of her position. She alone had had any real knowledge of the relationship that had led to this expedition. She had been witness when Vicky and Clarrie drove off down the lane. She knew where the lane was. Though she was the only one in the car who knew anything, the fact did not move her. She was dulled by lack of sleep though too uneasy to know how tired she was.

The police came back with the news that Clarrie Piper was not in his room. He had not returned to the house that night. No one there knew where he was.

Laura must now direct the police to the lane. The car went slowly. The moon glimmer gave wavering shape to the allotment huts, the brick kiln and the chimney.

The wall and the cottages loomed in the rusty light. 'This is where I waited,' she said but the place was unlike any place she had ever known. It was odd to think she had waited here so long.

'They left you and went on?' the sergeant asked.

'Yes. They turned a corner down there and went out of sight. I didn't see them after that.'

The car followed the bend and everyone watched through the windows as though at any moment Vicky and Clarrie might be seen lying or sitting or strolling under the trees. The pace was so slow, the car rocked on the ruts. For a mile they looked out on the same derelict orchard with the grotesque and broken trees and a scrub of elders and brambles. There was no movement anywhere. Mr Logan muttered in anguish: 'There's no sign of her. No sign.'

The headlights touched the sea-wall. The car came to a stop.

'What've we got here?' the sergeant asked.

'It's the hangar,' Laura said. 'Where they mended the sea-planes.'

The police left the car, each with a torch in his hand. 'You'd better come too, sir,' the sergeant said to Mr Logan.

Mr Logan opened the door beside him and leaving it open, followed the police across the marshy grass towards the hangar. A piece of broken canvas moved and rustled in the wind and the sound of it was unearthly in this forsaken place. Laura, seeing the men flashing the torch light over the blank black flank of the hangar, said: 'The door's on the other side. I must show them.'

'No. You stay here,' Mr Fletcher, hampered by his age and weight, tried to hold her but she slid away from him and was gone.

'The door's round here,' she shouted to the sergeant.

'We'll find it,' he assured her. 'You go back,' but she ran over the hard ridge to the door and pushed it open. She had meant merely to demonstrate her knowledge, expecting nothing, but the door fell in at a touch so she was the first to see Vicky. Vicky was on the platform, lying down, alone.

The tide was lapping in and the sheen from the water showed her legs stretched wide apart. Her arm was thrown towards the edge of the stage, her face turned to the sea.

Laura whispered: 'Vicky!'

The police, entering behind her, lit the scene with their torches so she could see that Vicky's eyes and mouth were open. Her dress had been torn down from the neck and she was bare to the waist. Seeing for the first time the exquisite whiteness of Vicky's bosom, Laura said in wonder: 'The breast of a swan.'

The sergeant stepped in front of her, blocking her view. 'Take that kid to the car,' he said angrily and the driver held her by the arm and led her past Mr Logan with his distorted face.

Meeting her father at the hangar door, she said: 'They've found Vicky.'

'What has happened?'

'I don't know.'

Mr Logan came out as though trying to escape suffoca-

182

tion and staring at Mr Fletcher, said hoarsely: 'How am I to tell my wife?'

Mr Fletcher was too moved to speak. Laura, putting her arm through his and leading him back to the car, noted her own poise and calm.

Leaving Mr Logan outside the hangar, the sergeant returned to the car to contact the Camperlea police station. He said into the radio telephone: 'We've found the Logan girl. Get on to the detective superintendent. We'll want the whole outfit: doctor, pathologist, scientific officer, cameras, the lot. I'll stay with the father. Yep, it looks like murder all right.'

The police car took the Fletchers home. Mr Fletcher, putting his arms round Laura and pressing her face to his pipe-reeking jacket, said: 'Poor Lory, you must be all in.' But Laura, in a feverish transport, felt intensely awake and aware as she contemplated the trick that had been played on her. The figure in the hangar had not been Vicky at all. It was too grotesque. Its pose was unnatural. It had been artificial, a manufactured object, like those dolls in the Play Room. 'The silliest sort of dolly dolls,' she thought with contempt.

Did they imagine she could be impeded by such a trick? No doubt her mother would use it to try and control her; and having offered the university, would now withdraw the offer.

'Let this be a lesson to you, Laura,' she would say. 'Nowadays girls think they can do anything but you see what happens!' It was intended to show her that for all their freedom, girls were vulnerable.

'Yet I will go,' she said aloud, speaking with such vehemence that her defences collapsed and reality flooded over her. Wherever she went, whatever she achieved, she would not have Vicky. That dazzling and enthralling love would not be given her again.

She drew her breath in with a sob and as her father pressed her to him, she whispered: 'I saw her. She was dead.'

She started to cry and all the way home, as her tears soaked into her father's coat, she sobbed: 'Vicky, Vicky, Vicky' as though the name, could she speak it with fervour enough, would bring her friend back, smiling, from the dead.

VIRAGO MODERN CLASSICS

The first Virago Modern Classic, *Frost in May* by Antonia White, was published in 1978. It launched a list dedicated to the celebration of women writers and to the rediscovery and reprinting of their works. Its aim was, and is, to demonstrate the existence of a female tradition in fiction which is both enriching and enjoyable. The Leavisite notion of the 'Great Tradition', and the narrow, academic definition of a 'classic', has meant the neglect of a large number of interesting secondary works of fiction. In calling the series 'Modern Classics' we do not necessarily mean 'great' — although this is often the case. Published with new critical and biographical introductions, books are chosen for many reasons: sometimes for their importance in literary history; sometimes because they illuminate particular aspects of women's lives, both personal and public. They may be classics of comedy or storytelling; their interest can be historical, feminist, political or literary.

Initially the Virago Modern Classics concentrated on English novels and short stories published in the early decades of this century. As the series has grown it has broadened to include works of fiction from different centuries, different countries, cultures and literary traditions. In 1984 the Victorian Classics were launched; there are separate lists of Irish, Scottish, European, American, Australian and other English speaking countries; there are books written by Black women, by Catholic and Jewish women, and a few relevant novels by men. There is, too, a companion series of Non-Fiction Classics constituting biography, autobiography, travel, journalism, essays, poetry, letters and diaries.

By the end of 1990 over 350 titles will have been published in these two series, many of which have been suggested by our readers.

THE DOVES OF VENUS
By Olivia Manning
New Introduction by Isobel English

"She opened her window and gazed down on the window of Margaretta Terrace ... What lay ahead for her? Would she ever rap on door-knockers with the urgency of important emotions? and run around a corner wearing a fur coat? and, lifting a hand to an approaching taxi, impress some other girl named Ellie and fill her with envy and ambition?"

Red-haired, eighteen-year-old Ellie leaves her home in the provincial seaside town of Eastsea and goes to London in search of independence, employment and experience. She finds a bedsit in Chelsea, a job painting "antique" furniture and a middle-aged lover called Quintin Bellot. Quintin's life is spent under the beady eye of his neurotic ex-wife Petta who haunts King's Road pubs with assorted Bohemians, nurturing virulent feelings towards Quintin's "little girls". And Ellie, having given her heart with the impetuosity of youth, gradually discovers the eternal complications of a love affair with a married man ...

Also of interest

RUTH ADAM
I'm Not Complaining

PHYLLIS SHAND ALLFREY
The Orchid House

ELIZABETH VON ARNIM
Elizabeth and Her German Garden
Fraulein Schmidt and Mr Anstruther
Vera

SYBILLE BEDFORD
A Compass Error
A Favourite of the Gods

ELIOT BLISS
Luminous Isle

ANGELA CARTER
The Magic Toyshop
The Passion of New Eve

BARBARA COMYNS
Our Spoons Came from Woolworths
Sisters by a River
The Vet's Daughter

JENNIFER DAWSON
The Ha-Ha

E. M. DELAFIELD
The Diary of a Provincial Lady

MAUREEN DUFFY
That's How It Was

EMILY EDEN
The Semi-Attached Couple
& The Semi-Detached House

GEORGE EGERTON
Keynotes and Discords

M. J. FARRELL (MOLLY KEANE)
Devoted Ladies
Mad Puppetstown
The Rising Tide
Two Days in Aragon

SARAH GRAND
The Beth Book

RADCLYFFE HALL
Adam's Breed
The Unlit Lamp
The Well of Loneliness

WINIFRED HOLTBY
Anderby Wold
The Crowded Street
The Land of Green Ginger
Mandoa, Mandoa!
Poor Caroline

STORM JAMESON
Company Parade
Love in Winter
None Turn Back
Women Against Men

ELIZABETH JENKINS
The Tortoise and the Hare

F. TENNYSON JESSE
The Lacquer Lady
Moonraker
A Pin to See the Peepshow

SHEILA KAYE-SMITH
Joanna Godden
Susan Spray

MARGARET KENNEDY
The Constant Nymph
The Ladies of Lyndon
Together and Apart
Troy Chimneys

MAURA LAVERTY
Never No More

ROSAMUND LEHMANN
The Ballad and the Source
The Gipsy's Baby
Invitation to the Waltz
A Note in Music
A Sea-Grape Tree
The Weather in the Streets

ADA LEVERSON
The Little Ottleys

ROSE MACAULAY
Told by an Idiot
The World My Wilderness

OLIVIA MANNING
The Doves of Venus
The Playroom

F. M. MAYOR
The Third Miss Symons

BETTY MILLER
On the Side of the Angels

NAOMI MITCHISON
The Corn King and the Spring Queen
Travel Light

EDITH OLIVIER
The Love Child

KATE O'BRIEN
Mary Lavelle
That Lady

JULIA O'FAOLAIN
Women in the Wall

MOLLIE PANTER-DOWNES
One Fine Day

MARY RENAULT
The Friendly Young Ladies

E. ARNOT ROBERTSON
Four Frightened People
Ordinary Families

VITA SACKVILLE-WEST
All Passion Spent
The Edwardians
No Signposts in the Sea

MAY SINCLAIR
Life and Death of Harriett Frean
Mary Olivier: A Life
The Three Sisters

STEVIE SMITH
The Holiday
Novel on Yellow Paper
Over the Frontier

LAURA TALBOT
The Gentlewomen

ELIZABETH TAYLOR
Angel
The Devastating Boys
In a Summer Season
Mrs Palfrey at the Claremont
Palladian
The Sleeping Beauty
The Soul of Kindness
The Wedding Group

VIOLET TREFUSIS
Hunt the Slipper

SYLVIA TOWNSEND WARNER
Mr Fortune's Maggot
The True Heart

MARY WEBB
The Golden Arrow
Gone to Earth
The House in Dormer Forest
Precious Bane
Seven for a Secret

REBECCA WEST
The Fountain Overflows
Harriet Hume
The Harsh Voice
The Judge
The Return of the Soldier
The Thinking Reed

ANTONIA WHITE
Beyond the Glass
Frost in May
The Lost Traveller
Strangers
The Sugar House

E. H. YOUNG
The Curate's Wife
Jenny Wren
Miss Mole
The Misses Mallett